"You do what I tell you."

"Come on. I want to fix the kid riding Champion."

"No!" said Ted. "I don't want to."

Jack grabbed Ted by the throat. His face was shiny and alive with hate. "You do what I tell you. You hear me?"

"I don't even know this kid. We might hurt him."

Jack grinned. It was the same grin Ted had seen that first evening near the mess hall, the same grin he had seen so many times since. Only now Jack was going to enjoy hurting this boy, in the same way he'd enjoyed beating up those kids at the haunted house and pushing Lee down in the watering trough. He was, Ted realized, capable of murder.

**Other Point Paperbacks
you will want to read:**

Take It Easy!
  by Steven Kroll

Don't Care High
  by Gordon Korman

Discontinued
  by Julian F. Thompson

Misjudged
  by Jeanette Mines

Deathman, Do Not Follow Me
  by Jay Bennett

Lure of the Dark
  by Sarah Sargent

point

BREAKING CAMP

Steven Kroll

SCHOLASTIC INC.
New York Toronto London Auckland Sydney

To my mother

ISBN 0-590-33795-5

12 11 10 9 8 7 6 5 4 3 2 1   7 8 9/8 0 1 2/9

Printed in the U.S.A.   01

First Scholastic printing, July 1987

ACKNOWLEDGMENTS

This book comes wrapped in thank-yous. To Karen Sacks for inspiration and for always coming up with the right answers. To my editor, Judith Whipple, for her sound criticism, commitment, and generosity of spirit. To my agent, Marilyn Marlow, and her assistants, Courtney Briggs and Scott Treimel, for being there when I needed them. And, for constant critical support, to George Blecher, Nancy Elghanayan, Tom Engelhardt, Elizabeth Levy, Beverly Lieberman, and Mara Miller.

One

When Ted Jenner got on the train at Penn Station that first Saturday morning in July, he had no idea what the summer would be like. A riding camp in Pennsylvania? His own horse to ride and look after? He'd never been to camp in his life.

Last summer, and every summer before that it seemed, he'd just hung out at his parents' country house in upstate New York. Played tennis. Gone riding and to the movies. Flirted with the girls downtown. He'd always enjoyed doing those things and having his own group of friends to do them with, but this summer he was fifteen. He would stay in the city, get a job, be responsible. Then his mother saw the ad for Camp Cherokee in the *New York Times*.

She thought he should go. "You've got your whole life to get a job," she said. "Why don't you just take this summer, get away, and have a good time!"

The ad showed the camp's logo, a leaping horse and rider, in the upper lefthand corner. Ted had always loved riding and been pretty good at it. He wasn't so sure he liked the idea that the camp was all boys, and the way of life seemed awfully rough and cut off from the outside world. But there were ways of rationalizing things like that. He'd recently broken up with his girlfriend, Lynn, and needed some time to cool it. A good, active summer of playing hard and learning about horses would be very refreshing. He'd be stronger physically. He might even make some new friends. By the time T. R. Bruce, the flinty, gray-haired director, had come by, shown his slides, and explained his devotion to the best Boy Scout camping traditions, Ted had decided to go.

And now here he was, waving good-bye to his parents on the platform and lurching down the aisle, trying to find a seat as the train gathered momentum and left the station behind.

A knot formed in his stomach. He didn't know a single person in the car. Everyone was wearing the same dumb uniform he was: green shirt, green and gold knit tie, khaki pants. He felt weird.

Tall, blond, usually graceful, Ted stumbled into a seat on the aisle, nearly dumping his duffel bag in the lap of a thin, dark boy by the window.

"Oh. Sorry," Ted said.

The boy smiled. "That's okay."

Ted disentangled the duffel bag, stowed it in the rack above the seat, and sat down hard.

"Whew," he said, wiping a shock of blond hair out of his eyes. "That was like walking a tightrope without the rope." He held out his hand. "Ted Jenner."

"Lee Fischer," said the boy, and held out his.

"Where are you from, Lee Fischer?"

"The Island. Port Washington."

"What's it like living out there? Long Island always seemed like one big shopping mall to me."

"We've got a big house. And grass. And clean air."

2

"Sounds pretty nice."

The train emerged into daylight. Ted leaned back and relaxed. The school year had turned out really well. He'd boosted his average to a B+. He'd been elected captain of the soccer team for next fall. No junior had ever been made captain before. And if he stuck with student government, he might even get to be president. He wasn't even missing Lynn much anymore. They really hadn't been getting along anyway.

Lee asked him where he was from, and he said, "The City."

"Everyone always told me New York was full of muggers and dirt and thieves."

"It is," said Ted, "and I love it."

Lee laughed nervously. He pulled at the knot in his tie.

Ted pointed at the round, gold patch on the pocket of Lee's shirt. Everyone had one of these patches, with a number in the middle.

"You've been coming to Cherokee for *five* summers?"

"Yup," said Lee. "I'm what you might call a distinguished, older camper."

"Do they give you a medal after so many years or something?"

"No. They just seem to like it if you keep coming back."

"Why do you?"

Lee stumbled over his words. "I love the horses," he said quickly, "and the mountains."

Ted couldn't figure this kid out. He seemed smart and interesting, but sort of wimpy. "Is there anything you don't like?" he asked.

A flood seemed to have been released. "Oh, God, yes,"

3

said Lee. "There are these inspections every morning, and on Saturdays they make you go skinny dipping in the lake at six-thirty A.M. After the skinny dip, there's something called Director's Inspection because T. R. Bruce, the director, does the inspecting, and that's a real bitch. Clean fingernails, bouncing a quarter on your bed, that sort of stuff. Then there's this whole competition thing. Win or lose, win or lose, all the time. I think T. R. would give an award for who ate the fastest in the mess hall if he could."

Some of this Ted had heard from Mr. Bruce himself, but not quite in this way. "Doesn't sound like a place you'd want to come back to."

"Oh, there's more. There's a camp fraternity called the Cherokee Tribe, and no one's supposed to know who the members are or what they do. I think it's run by this really nasty kid, Jack Dunn, and I think they do a whole lot of mean stuff out at the haunted houses and places like that."

"Haunted houses?"

"Yeah. Mr. Bruce leads groups of kids out to these deserted, old houses in the middle of the night. Then he grades you on how scared you get. Sounds terrific, huh?"

This was all new stuff. No one had mentioned anything about the Cherokee Tribe or haunted houses. But who could tell? It might turn out to be fun.

"I don't understand. There's so much you don't like. Why don't you go somewhere else?"

Lee seemed to retreat into himself. He smiled. "Cherokee's the best riding camp in the East. If you want to be around horses, it's the place to be."

At that moment Higg appeared.

Higg was Luther G. Higgins, Head Counselor, Horseman

Division, and director of the camp riding program. He was tall and bald, and, in his riding breeches and boots, with a pipe stuck in his shirt pocket, he looked both tough and distinguished.

When Higg had introduced himself and learned that Ted was going to be a Horseman, he hitched up his pants and said, "Well, it's nice to have some new blood. Gets a little tiresome seeing the same old faces year after year."

Ted laughed. "From what Lee's been telling me, Cherokee campers have to be dragged away by the heels."

Higg nodded. "I guess it isn't every camp that offers you your own horse for the summer. Of course not every boy would be up to it, but I like to think of our Horsemen as something special."

He had a reedy, raspy voice.

Ted asked, "If the Horsemen have their own horses, when do the other kids get to ride?"

"It's not quite what you've been thinking," Higg said. "You won't be spending all day every day in the saddle. You'll have a full program of camp activities just like everyone else. The other kids will ride an hour every day, and so will you. You'll just have the added responsibility of looking after your horse. If you're good, you'll go on extra overnights."

"Sounds fine to me."

Higg smiled. "I thought it would. Glad I stopped by."

He shook Ted's hand—a firm shake—and returned to his seat.

Ted basked in the glow of this meeting. Lee had almost disappeared into his corner by the window.

"Hey," Ted said, "what's with you and Higg?"

"Oh, nothing," said Lee. "We just don't like each other much."

"How can you not get along with the guy who runs the division?"

"I manage."

"But what's the problem?"

Lee shrugged. "I think he's weak."

"That man who just shook my hand and walked away as if he owned the train?"

"That man everyone thinks is the epitome of fairness and the best teacher—of riding or anything else—they ever had."

"I don't get it."

"You don't have to."

"But—"

"I'd just as soon not talk about it anymore."

"Oh," said Ted. "Okay."

He turned to the window. Suburban tacky was becoming the rich, full green of country fields. He could feel the summer coming closer, a mellowing in the air, and a deepening of his curiosity over just what Camp Cherokee might be like.

"What horse did you choose?" he asked.

"Flash," said Lee. "I've wanted him for years. He's this big buckskin gelding with a white blaze and four white socks. He's fast and tough, and Jack Dunn almost fixed it so I wouldn't—"

"You've really got problems with some of these people."

"I'm sorry," Lee said. "I didn't want to sound like that."

"You're sure you don't want to talk about it?"

"No, that's okay. Maybe some other time. What horse did you get?"

"Nelly."

"Oh, God. Nelly. Those pictures they send you new guys, they never show enough. All the good horses were taken by the end of last summer."

Ted felt stung. "What's the matter with Nelly?"

"Oh, she's okay. She's just very highstrung. Maybe you can straighten her out."

"Well," said Ted, "I guess I'll give it my best shot."

He got up to go to the bathroom, waved and got a wave back from Higg as he passed the endless rows of green and gold and khaki-clad figures. When he returned, a box lunch was waiting.

Lee was all smiles. "I saved it for you."

"Thanks," said Ted.

This kid could be as nice as he was irritating.

They ate silently, balancing the boxes on their knees. Then Lee said, "By the way, what bunk are you in?"

The train lurched. Ted grabbed his container of milk. "Horseman Division, Cabin 3."

"Hey," said Lee, "I can't believe it. I'm in Cabin 3, too!"

Two

Camp Cherokee sat on a hill. The Old Glory Road ran through it. To the left were the official camp buildings— mess hall, canteen, administration, infirmary—and in front of them a vast sweep of green with cabins along the edge. To the right was a large riding field and corral. Below the riding field, at the bottom of the hill, were the stable and the pasture, and way over on the other side, past the cabins and a half-mile deep into the woods, was the lake.

Everything about the place seemed wide open and spacious, and yet, at the same time, there was something totally contained about it. Sure, you could wander over to the riding field or down to the stable or across the vast green lawn to the cabins, but beyond those limits—beyond the perfectly cut grass, the perfectly polished cabins and camp buildings—was an alien world, a world you would be kept from entering.

Stay here with us, the very beauty and orderliness of the camp seemed to proclaim. Put away your thoughts of home and family. Forget the loose ends of your other life. While you are here, we will be your reality. And for good measure, there was no sign of a TV antenna anywhere, no sign of a newspaper on a porch or the sound of a radio playing.

The message seemed to be that Cherokee was yours but

you were also Cherokee's, and there were very private rules to follow, rules you would learn soon enough. Until you got home, you could ignore those rules at your peril.

Thoughts like this wandered in and out of Ted's head as the green camp GMC pulled up in front of the administration building. Heaving his bag out of the back, he couldn't be sure if he felt more ambivalent about the camp or about having Lee Fischer as a bunkmate.

They had gone on talking for the rest of the trip. Most of the conversation—about schoolwork, and sports, and books—had seemed perfectly friendly. But every so often, Lee had said something—usually about a person at camp— that sounded odd or resentful.

Identical with all the others, Cabin 3, Horseman Division, looked like a spruced-up version of something Abe Lincoln might have lived in. Ted and Lee walked up the three steps and went inside. They ran right into Hambone Hamilton.

"Lee, baby!" said Hambone, stretching his huge arms wide. "I didn't know you were in this bunk. How ya doin'?"

"Oh, fine, Hambone," said Lee. "When did you get in?"

"My folks dropped me off about an hour ago. I stopped off at the barn to see Jim and Jake."

Six feet tall and two hundred pounds, Hambone wasn't fat so much as he was large. His commanding presence, so good-humored and almost adult, seemed, however critically, to allow anybody in. But Ted couldn't tell if he was glad to see Lee or not. His words seemed sincere enough, but somehow touched with disappointment.

"Who's your friend?" Hambone said. "And why don't I know him?"

9

"He's new," said Lee. "I met him on the train."

When they had been introduced, Ted said, "And who are Jim and Jake?"

"My illegitimate children," said Hambone, and laughed a deep, throaty laugh. "No, seriously, they're a team of workhorses. I drive the camp covered wagon, and they pull it. Take the little kids on overnight trips to Crescent Lake. The kids who aren't old enough to go on horseback overnights."

"Must be a nice job."

"Can't beat it. Hours are pretty much my own, I get out of a lot of bullshit camp activities, and at Crescent Lake I've got all the comforts. Get to sleep in the wagon instead of on the cold ground. Even make a little money on the side."

"Money?" said Ted. "Aren't you a camper?"

"Sure, but there are always tips from grateful parents. My real name's Jesse, by the way. Everyone just calls me Hambone."

"You should cut us all in," said Lee. "Make sure you've got protection."

Hambone laughed. "Not so fast, wise guy."

Ted didn't think Hambone was annoyed, but now Lee was saying, very defensively, "Sorry, Hambone, you know I was just joking. How was your winter? How did school go?"

"Well, I managed to pass all my courses. When I wasn't passing out from the booze, that is. I'm sure I don't have to ask how you did, you little overachiever."

"I did okay," Lee said.

"And how about you?" said Hambone, looking over at Ted.

"Oh, I just hung in," said Ted. "I played a lot of soccer and mixed it up in student government."

"Hey!" said Hambone, "an extracurricular type. Bound to be useful. Wouldn't you say, Fischer?"

"Oh, sure," Lee said.

"You could be more enthusiastic."

"I *am* enthusiastic," said Lee. "I *like* Ted already. Can't you guys get off my case?"

"We're not on your case," said a voice from the rear of the cabin. "We're on your back."

Hambone chuckled.

"Who's that?" said Lee.

"Who do you think?" said the voice.

The cabin was the size of one modest bedroom. Hung down the middle was a pole for clothes. On either side were two bunk beds. Near the door was the counselor's bed. Now, from behind some clothes draped over the pole, came the most perfect baby face—clear blue eyes, pug nose, close-cropped blond hair—that Ted had ever seen.

The face smiled. "Surprise."

"Tim Fairchild!" said Lee.

"Well, who did you expect? Billy the Kid?"

"That would have been interesting."

"I'd rather be me," said Tim.

He stepped out from behind the clothes. He was medium height and wearing perfectly faded jeans, a T-shirt, and running shoes.

Ted introduced himself.

Tim gave him the once-over, and Ted knew right away this kid was trouble. He was the sort of kid who did things effortlessly, who had charm and smarts and never got dirty. He would never be a real leader, but he would always be effortlessly popular. And yet, because he would never be a leader, he would always be lacking in a certain kind of confidence. And because he lacked that confidence, he would strike out at weaker kids—the ones it was easy to make fun of. He would also find any competition threatening. Ted Jenner was one of those kids who found it easy to be popular and could be a leader, too. Tim Fairchild knew that already. Ted Jenner was the competition! And Tim would do anything not to be upstaged.

"Well, Tim," said Hambone, "what's the verdict?"

Tim laughed. "I guess he'll pass. He's certainly a cut above Fischer."

"Is this really necessary?" Ted said.

"Hey, look what we've got," said Tim. "Mr. High-and-Mighty."

"I'm not Mr. *anything*," Ted said, "but give us a break. We only just got here."

Tim's smile was back. "You know, you're right. I'm sorry. Why don't the two of you choose your bunks, and we'll go from there."

Ted didn't believe a word of this apology, but he said, "Sure, what's available?"

"Well," said Tim, "Hambone's got that bottom one, and I've got the top. So there's a top and a bottom left."

"I guess I'd like the top."

"Would you mind?" said Lee. "I really wanted the top."

"Now come on, don't be like that," said Hambone. "Ted's never been to Cherokee before. Let him have his choice."

"I had a bottom bunk all last summer," said Lee.

"Look," said Ted, "I really don't care which bunk I have.

The bottom one will do fine."

"Ridiculous," said Tim. "You said you'd like that top bunk, and I don't see why you shouldn't have it. Lee's had his chance. So what if he had a bottom bunk last year?"

Knowing how hostile Tim had been, Ted was surprised he'd become his great defender, even if it did mean getting more satisfying licks in at Lee.

"This is too much," Lee said.

He spun around and left the cabin. Ted went after him. He found him in the woods, hands on hips.

He tapped him on the shoulder.

Lee flinched. "Leave me alone."

"Look," said Ted, "we're going to make a deal."

"Deal? Why would you want to make a deal with me?"

"Because I only just met you, and I'd like the summer to begin on a pleasant—"

"Yeah. Me too!" said Lee. "That's all I ever want. Just the chance to begin the summer pleasantly. And it never happens!"

He whirled around and faced Ted. Tears stained his cheeks, and he kept looking between the cabins, as if someone were going to appear and embarrass him at any moment. "*That's* why I keep coming back. It's more than just the horses and the mountains. I keep thinking that each summer I'll be able to begin again, that I can be liked and accepted just like anyone else. I guess I must be crazy. Jack Dunn ruined that chance long ago."

"Jack Dunn? Isn't he the kid you mentioned on the train?"

"Yup. One and the same. He's the one who really runs this place."

13

"But he's just another camper."

"Weird, isn't it. You'll see how things work soon enough."

"But what did Jack Dunn ever do to you?"

"First summer I was here, he decided he didn't like me. I never knew why exactly. He just decided. Then he told all the other guys not to like me either, to stay away, so they did. And that's the way it's been, summer after summer. I can't even get a top bunk if I want it!"

"I guess, after all that, I wouldn't bother coming back."

"But I do like it here! I like the horses and the mountains. I like being an old camper. I guess I just wish Jack wouldn't come back. I know that isn't very likely, and who can say if it would even make any difference. Tim and Hambone, they're great pals of Jack's. They'd probably hate me anyway. But—oh, I don't know. . . ."

Lee grabbed at a branch and held onto it. He turned his head away.

Ted didn't know exactly what to believe. Everything Lee said seemed a little too farfetched. But there wasn't any way to figure it out now. All he could do was try to solve the problem at hand.

"About that deal," Ted said. "I don't really care if you have that top bunk or not, but I'm going to tell those guys in there we've reached a compromise. You'll have it the first half of the summer. I'll have it the second half. We just won't remember to switch."

Lee looked right at him. "You'd do that for me?"

"Sure. It's nothing."

"I think it's something. Thank you."

Ted shrugged. "Well, forget it. Now let's tell the others

before someone thinks I've chased you out of camp."

When they got back inside, Doug Parelli, their counselor, had arrived. Doug was a big, red-faced, easygoing guy, a high-school teacher from Philadelphia.

Leaning back against his pillow, hands behind his head, he said, "How close are we to a solution?"

"We've got one," Ted said.

Doug smiled. "Hear that, guys? Sometimes the new kids do better than the best campers."

Tim, sitting on his upper bunk, looked as if he'd been slapped.

"Best camper?" Ted said.

Hambone laughed. "Tim was our Horseman best camper last year. All the counselors voted. Even Doug Parelli. Didn't you, Doug?"

"I won't deny it. And I wasn't even bribed."

"Gosh," said Tim, obviously hurt again. "What a tribute."

"Just keeping you on your toes, Fairchild. Now Mr. Jenner, though we haven't been properly introduced, I'd like to hear your solution."

Oh, boy, Ted thought. This kid Tim's so insecure, I'm even more of a threat to him than I imagined. He explained the bunk arrangements.

"Perfect," Hambone, said. "How'd you like to help me out with my parents?"

Ted smiled. "I'd be delighted. As long as they both don't come out swinging at once."

"Guaranteed," said Hambone. "We lock my dad in the hall closet every night at nine."

"What a good idea," said Doug, "but I prefer the dog-

15

house. Which is where you guys are going to be if you don't get yourselves unpacked and ready for flag-lowering. Good work, Ted. Now move your butts. All of you."

Three

A loud, crackling sound followed by the scratching of a needle on an old record. Suddenly—bursting out over the camp—a bugle call, loud and piercing. Assembly. Line up at the flagpole.

Ted stowed a towel in the cubbyhole beside his bed, shut the lid of his trunk, and headed for the door. The rest of his bunkmates were right behind him.

Only Doug Parelli was left in the cabin. He stuck his head out. "Hey, you guys. I'm supposed to tell you it's time for the flag. What's a counselor for?"

Hambone waved. "Come on, Dougie. If you're good, we'll save you a place in line. Maybe you'll even get to have dinner."

"Oh, boy," shouted Doug. "Wait for me."

Everyone was in uniform. The boys from the train had kept theirs on. The boys who'd been driven up by their parents had changed. Ted had to wear a tie to school every day in New York. It seemed very odd to be wearing one in the middle of the Blue Ridge Mountains. Still, all of this green and gold and khaki descending on the flagpole in the near dark looked impressive. And at least they'd be back in jeans and T-shirts after dinner.

The groups fanned out. Juniors. Intermediates. Seniors.

17

Horsemen. Standing in the line for Cabin 3, with Tim and Lee in front and Hambone behind, Ted watched Higg and T. R. Bruce prepare to bring down the flag.

They were thin and about the same height, but where Higg was wiry and slightly stooped, Mr. Bruce was all taut muscle. Everything about him was gray, from his cropped hair and keen eyes to the strange pallor of his skin.

He welcomed everyone to Camp Cherokee. "Ordinarily," he said, "you campers will be chosen, on a weekly basis, to raise and lower the flag. But tonight, because it is the first night, Mr. Higgins and I will do the honors."

Rule number one of how many? As the bugle began to play over the public-address system and the Stars and Stripes came slowly down the pole, Ted gazed out around the lines of campers and counselors, noticing small boys with terrified, homesick faces, boys standing flat-footed and bored, counselors looking earnest and resigned, and far over on the left, at the very edge of the Horsemen group, one dark figure.

Ted could hardly take his eyes off him. He was so dark, so intense, he seemed to gather everyone's energy into himself. Standing there, even in repose, he made Ted nervous.

The flag came down and was folded into the correct triangles. The bugle call ended and was replaced with something that sounded like "Come and get your beans, boys, come and get your beans." The group around the flagpole dispersed and headed for the mess hall with audible relief.

Though he usually felt at home anywhere, Ted had a moment of disorientation. He was in a totally isolated, strange place, surrounded by unfamiliar people. The air smelled sweet but very different. The crickets were chirping suspiciously. It was almost dark and growing colder.

Walking toward the mess hall, he didn't feel like talking to anyone. Suddenly someone was talking to him.

"Hi," the voice said. "New, aren't you? Jack Dunn's the name."

It was the boy Ted had noticed, only now he didn't seem intense at all. He was tall and loose-limbed, with smooth, delicate features. Open and friendly, his brown eyes flashed. He grinned.

"Glad to meet you," Ted said. "I'm Ted Jenner. You're right. This is my first summer here."

"Had to be," said Jack. "I know my Horsemen."

"*Your* Horsemen?"

"Just a figure of speech. You know. Anyhow, I wanted to welcome you aboard. Hope I'll see more of you, and all that stuff."

"I appreciate it."

The brown eyes flashed again. So did the grin. "Yeah, well, that's me. Don't want you new guys feeling neglected."

"How long have you been at Cherokee?"

"Seven seasons. Started as a Junior. But a Horseman's what you want to be."

"Yes, I know. What do the other campers do for self-esteem?"

"Dream about being Horsemen."

Ted laughed. "I guess I'm pretty lucky. Hit the bull's eye first time out."

"You sure are," said Jack. "Look, I gotta go, but I'll see you later. Just watch out for the chow. It could do in a stomach made of stone."

"Okay," Ted said. "Thanks for the warning."

19

Already he was feeling more welcome. There was something so beguiling about this kid Dunn. He just put you at your ease right away. Ted could even forgive him that "my Horsemen" remark. After seven summers at one camp, anyone would think he owned the place. On the other hand, there was all that dark intensity he'd noticed before, such a contradiction of what he'd just experienced.

Wait a minute. Jack Dunn. That was the kid Lee said had been so cruel to him. Was that possible? This smiling, friendly kid? And what about running the camp? Were the Horsemen really *his* Horsemen? By the time Ted reached the mess hall, his mind was racing.

The building was cavernous, and the food as dreadful as Jack had predicted. Some sort of weird chicken croquette-like thing, breaded and deep fried, together with boiled-to-mush potatoes and dry succotash. He could have done without any of it, but was too hungry to start making judgments. He helped himself to a portion of each.

Lee refused to take potatoes.

"Come on," said Doug, "this isn't the Juniors. Everyone has something of everything."

Hambone went to grab the platter. As he grabbed it, it slipped out of his hands and tumbled into Lee's lap. "Whoops," said Hambone. "Sorry, I didn't mean to do that."

Lee stood up, slopping potatoes into his napkin and wiping at his khakis at the same time. It was hard to tell if he felt Hambone had dumped the platter on purpose or not.

He sat down. He took the spoon from the potatoes and served himself a small portion of what was left.

"Good," said Doug.

"Would someone please pass the salt and pepper."

"Local or express?" said Tim.

"Local," said Lee.

Tim shot the salt and pepper shakers across the table into Lee's lap.

"Did I hear you right?" said Tim. "I was sure you said express."

When the dessert had been served, a particularly nasty cherry Jello with fruit in it, someone knocked on a glass with a spoon. The entire mess hall went quiet as T. R. Bruce got up to speak.

He stood there at the microphone, all grayness and severity. For a moment it seemed as if he wouldn't say anything at all, as if he'd just stand there admiring the quiet. Then he began.

And it was boring. A speech about the heritage of Camp Cherokee and the camp's devotion to excellence, discipline, Boy Scout traditions, and fair play. These virtues, he said, were to be expressed in everything a Cherokee camper did, and he hoped there would be enough going on during the summer to make expressing them both worthwhile and entertaining. There was stuff about different counselors and different activities and about the centerpiece of those activities: Higg's prestigious riding program. There was also a reference to Parents' Weekend and to some "special events" that were not named. Mr. Bruce smiled devilishly at that phrase "special events." Ted figured that at least one of them had to be the haunted-house trips Lee had been talking about.

Finally there was an end, as rousing a call for camp spirit and camp loyalty as Mr. Bruce could muster in that monotone voice of his. "And don't forget," he said, "for all of you, for new and old campers alike, we wish you a summer you will remember all your lives."

He sat down. Everyone stamped and cheered and whistled. But Ted did not. That strange feeling of isolation had come over him again. Mr. Bruce had made no mention of the world outside. He seemed concerned about camp activities and nothing else. And what he described sounded so rigid and predetermined, as if the good time had been squeezed out of it already.

Mr. Bruce hadn't really said anything different from what he'd said in the city. It was just that here, with imagination giving way to reality, his words had a different effect. Ted folded his arms over his chest. In the huge mess hall, he felt stifled.

The evening air was crisp and promising, but a little too cool for a shirt and tie without a jacket. Walking back to the cabins, kids divided up into small groups. Ted fell back, wondering if, despite his reservations, this really would be a summer he would remember all his life. He thought of hurrying to rejoin his bunkmates, then decided against it. He'd see them back at the cabin.

He started across the field. Suddenly Lee was at his side. They walked together in silence. Then Ted said, "I think you overdo it sometimes."

"You mean refusing the potatoes?"

"The potatoes. And the bunks. And Hambone."

"I know. Something just comes over me. I dig in and get stubborn. But a lot of it's not my fault. It's what I told you—"

"You mean Jack Dunn?"

"Yes."

22

"I met Jack coming to the mess hall. He was weird, but he seemed like a nice guy."

"He's not. He's a menace!"

"He was pretty nice to me."

"He's trying to suck up to you. He probably wants to use you."

"Why would he want to use me? He just wanted to make me feel comfortable."

Lee stopped short. He had turned very red. His eyes were wide. "Because he uses everyone! And he'll turn you against me, too!"

"Lee!"

"I'm sorry," Lee said. "But I can't help telling you the truth."

"Don't you think I can make up my own mind about that?"

"No! You shouldn't have to. If you don't want to be my friend, you don't need to be!"

"Well, thanks a lot."

"You're welcome!"

It was enough. Ted marched into the cabin.

Four

The poker game was already underway when Ted walked in and sat down. Doug was dealing to Hambone and Tim. It took only a moment for Ted to become part of the action and only another moment for Lee to creep up to his bunk. The air was filled with the sound of slapping cards.

"Hot damn!" said Hambone. "Look at this hand."

"I don't believe it," said Ted. "You beat my two pair. I thought you were bluffing."

"Me?" said Hambone. "The king of hands, bluffing?"

"Never," said Tim. "How could we forget? The king of hands should never be confused with an ace-hole. Right, Doug?"

Tim laughed. Doug laughed, too. Even Hambone began to laugh. "Not bad, Timmy," he said. "Not bad for a bullshit best camper."

"Thanks, Hambone," said Tim. "Maybe I'll even win a hand from you one of these years."

"Well, I'm game for that right now," said Ted. "Deal the cards, Tim. It's your turn, isn't it?"

"No, stop, put the cards away," said Doug.

"Hey, what's going on?" said Hambone.

"Nothing's going on. It's time for canteen. Remember canteen, Hambone? Your favorite sport? If you guys don't get up there in the next ten minutes, you'll miss your turn."

"Why didn't you say so?" said Hambone. "Ted. Tim. Off your butts!"

"I'm not really hungry," said Ted. "Maybe I'll just stay here."

"Bullshit," said Hambone. "We'll find you something irresistible. Right, Tim?"

"Oh. Sure," said Tim, forcing a smile.

"Well, don't fall all over yourself, Timmy," Hambone said. "Come on, Ted. Come with us."

"Well, okay," Ted said.

"Hang on a minute," Tim said. "I forgot my coupon book."

Hambone and Ted slouched by the cabin door, waiting. Then the three of them tumbled out.

A moment later Ted was back.

"Hey, Lee," he said to the rafters, "you coming to canteen?"

Lee's head turned on his bunk. "What?"

"Are you coming to canteen?"

Ted could feel the smile spread over Lee's face.

"Coming? Sure I'm coming. Just a second."

All the way across the field, Ted couldn't get over Lee's enthusiasm.

"I think I'll have a frozen Milky Way," he said. "No, maybe a Clark Bar or a Planter's Peanut Block. I just can't make up my mind. What are you going to have, Ted?"

"God knows," said Ted. "Maybe just a fit."

He had gone back for him out of guilt. He'd also wanted to give him another chance. Hambone and Tim hadn't been interested, but when he'd said he didn't think it was

25

right to leave him, they had shrugged and said okay.

About ten people were ahead of them at the canteen window. They slipped in behind Hambone and Tim.

Four ahead, then two, then Tim: "A pint of maple walnut and a Snickers bar, please."

"Good choice," said Hambone. "I'll have the same."

They paid. Lee was next.

"I'd like a pint of maple walnut and a Snickers," Lee said.

"My," said Tim, digging into his maple walnut, "that's original."

"Sorry," said the clerk, who was one of the mess hall waiters doing overtime, "all out of maple walnut."

Lee looked stunned, as if, somehow, this wrong had been done to him personally. "But they"—he pointed at Hambone and Tim—"they just bought—"

"Those were the last ones. Can I help you with something else?"

"Yes," snapped Lee. "I'll have a pint of vanilla, and skip the Snickers."

He took the ice cream and walked over to Hambone and Tim. Ted still didn't feel like anything to eat, but since he was there and it was his turn, he decided to have the Snickers bar Lee had abandoned. When he had paid for it and joined his three bunkmates in the shadows, he discovered a quarrel in progress.

"Lee asked us if we'd trade some of our maple walnut for his vanilla," Hambone said.

"But I don't like vanilla," said Tim.

"Vanilla is boring," said Hambone.

"So you said no," said Ted.

"Yes," said Hambone. "We said no."

"And Lee got pissed," said Tim.

"I wouldn't have bought the vanilla if I didn't think they'd share with me," said Lee.

"Now wait just a minute," Ted said.

"I'm going back to the bunk," said Lee.

Ted was speechless. All three of them had been wrong, and he had wanted to say that. But Lee had been totally impossible. Jack or no Jack, no wonder he didn't have any friends! Now there was no point in saying anything.

He chewed on a piece of Snickers bar. "What are you guys doing now?"

There was a silence.

"I don't know about Tim," said Hambone, "but I'm going to finish my ice cream and turn in."

"I guess I'll do the same," said Tim.

At least the argument was over. Ted finished the Snickers bar and threw the wrapper in the garbage. "I think I'll go check out the stars for a while. See you back at the bunk."

"Okay," said Hambone.

"See you," said Tim, without enthusiasm.

The tennis courts were wrapped in calm. He leaned against the fence, taking it all in. The cabin lights. The stars that had never looked so bright. The sweep of sky just above the shadows of the trees. It was good to be alone. He stuck his hands in the pockets of his sweatshirt.

A noise to his right. He peered into the darkness. There it was again, the scrunching of gravel on the path.

Then a voice: "Hey! Ted Jenner!"

Ted spun around. The voice had come from the opposite

direction. The sound of running feet. More scrunching of gravel.

"Hey, Jenner!"

Ted spun around again. The voice seemed everywhere at once.

A figure jumped out of the shadows. The loose-limbed stance. The grin. The same voice, softer: "Hi, Ted!"

Ted was dumfounded. "Hi, Jack. What's all this sneaking around?"

"Thought I'd impress you with my tracking skills in the wild. Were you impressed?"

Ted laughed. "Not very."

"Pity. How about a candy bar instead?"

He threw Ted a Snickers bar. Ted caught it and handed it back. "No, thanks. I just finished one of these."

"How'd you like to do better?"

"I'm not sure what you mean."

"Follow me and find out."

"Do I want to?"

"Only you can answer that."

Jack started to walk away. Ted watched him saunter around the edge of the tennis courts. What sort of weird invitation was this?

Jack stopped and waved. Ted could see the grin and the slouch through the dark. It was impossible not to be curious. Oh, hell, he thought. You only live once.

He strolled over. Jack said, "I thought you'd come. I don't usually make the wrong choices."

Ted bristled. This guy was so damn full of assumptions. "Well, I'm here."

Jack set out across the field. He disappeared into the

woods at the edge of the Intermediate cabins. There was a path. It was narrow and dark, but he had no trouble finding it without a flashlight. Ted was behind him all the way.

As they thrust their way through the woods, parting tree branches and jumping logs where necessary, Jack began to talk.

"You know," he said, "we're a very special little group here at Cherokee. We're sort of responsible for a lot that gets done and for a certain tone that's established. And every year I make a very careful point of choosing a handful, sometimes much less than a handful, of new campers to join our inner circle."

He went on like this for a while, as the path twisted and turned and the woods grew thicker. Ted was intrigued and bothered at the same time. He remembered what Lee had said about Jack and the Cherokee Tribe, but this didn't seem to be about the Tribe. He liked Jack's style, and that was enough for a start. But all this mysterious stuff made him seem spookier and weirder than ever.

Suddenly there was a clearing and a campfire. Around the campfire, leaning against trees and lying on the ground, were some boys. They were drinking beer and dragging on joints.

Three of them Ted didn't know. The other two were Hambone and Tim.

He was surprised. "I thought you guys were going to sleep."

Hambone looked up. He passed the joint to Tim. "Oh, yeah. But we remembered Jack usually has a little something going the first night of camp. Soooo—"

Ted didn't know whether or not to be disappointed or

29

offended. Had they lied to him, or did it even matter? Jack had included him. Take it from there.

Jack said, "I see you know a few of the guys. You'll have to meet the others."

"I'm glad you're here," said Hambone, smiling through the smoke.

"What do you *want?*" said Tim.

His big blue eyes were looking straight at Ted. They were not smiling. They were telling him he was not welcome, that he had become too popular too fast and was getting in Tim's way.

"How's that?" said Ted.

Jack was pushing him forward, his face gleaming in the firelight.

"Welcome, man. This is the place to be."

Ted wasn't so very sure. Not yet. Lee might be absolutely infuriating, but could he be right about this guy?

"Do you want a beer or a joint?" said Tim.

"I'll have a beer," said Ted, and sat down.

Five

Hands shaking him. Shaking him again.

"Hey, lay off," he said. "Come on. Let me sleep."

He tried to turn over on his side, but the hands wouldn't let him. He fought with the hands, but they insisted.

"Ted," the voice said, "it's after six. You've got to get going."

"What?" he said. "What time?"

He sat up and saw Lee's thin, smiling face. "It's late," Lee said. "If you're not at the riding field by six-thirty, they'll probably throw you in the watering trough."

They? They? Who were they? Were they counselors? Were they Jack and his group? He remembered last night, coming in late and falling into bed. Oh, what a headache. Why had he decided to become a Horseman? He hated getting up at this hour, sleep or no sleep, was hopeless before nine or ten. Besides, it was cold and damp out there. He pulled the covers over his head.

Lee laughed and yanked the covers off. Ted was scrunched up in a ball, eyes closed tight, arms crossed.

"Come on," Lee said. "Really."

Ted twitched. He opened his eyes. Then he jumped out of bed, pulled his robe on over his pajamas, and found his moccasins.

"I'll be back," he said.

The latrine was out behind the cabins. There were two for the Horseman Division, each equipped with rows of sinks, urinals, and stalls. Oh, my God, was it cold going through the woods. And it was so early, his pajama pants were soaked with dew in a minute. When he got back, Lee was waiting.

"Why didn't you go?" Ted said. "You'll get in trouble."

"Only if I'm late." He smiled again. "Someone had to get you out of here in time."

"You're too much," Ted said. Too much and what else? he thought as he pulled on his jeans and boots. Was this kid just trying to get points after last night?

When they reached the riding field, most of the other Horsemen were already hanging out around the corral. Ted nodded hello. He was pleased that everyone looked as sleepy as he felt. But where was Jack? Didn't he have to show up like anyone else?

Suddenly Jack was there, standing on the watering trough, signaling for quiet.

"I'm glad to see you're all here on time," he said, flashing a grin. "Higg has asked me to tell you about a new rule we'll be enforcing this summer."

A *new* rule? thought Ted. And what was this "*we'll* be enforcing" business? Ted looked over at Higg, but Higg was just puffing on his pipe.

Jack went on. "You know how some of you guys are always loafing between the riding field and the stable? Well, from now on, we *run* from the riding field to get the horses. And during the day, after we've brought them down, we *run* back. That's every time. And the person who's last gets thrown in the trough, the one down there or the one up here."

Everyone groaned.

"What's the matter?" said Jack. "Isn't everybody happy?"

"Don't we have enough to do?" someone shouted.

"I'm really surprised at you guys," Jack said. "Where's your Horseman spirit, your all-American get-up-and-go?"

Someone else shouted, "What's the point, Jack?"

A few others applauded lightly. "Yeah, what's the point?" spread around the group.

Jack folded his arms. "The point, gentlemen, is to toughen you up! Get going!"

He pointed down the hill. At first no one knew what to do. Then a couple of guys took a few steps, and suddenly everyone was running! Forty Horsemen running for dear life.

Ted ran so hard, he thought his lungs would burst. Across the riding field and down the hill. There was a path for the horses, but it was narrow and no one used it, just spilling down the hillside and heading for the barns instead.

He was somewhere near the middle of the pack. With everyone panicking, he'd lost track of Lee and Hambone, wasn't really aware of anyone but himself, running, running so as not to lose. He crossed the hardtop road at the bottom of the hill and made it to the stable. The watering trough was beside the entrance to the pasture. He collapsed in front of it.

Jack breezed in after him. What do you know! Jack had run, too. And there were Lee and Tim, and then Hambone,

33

lumbering in almost but not quite last.

There was a squeal, loud and high-pitched, like an angry piglet.

"It's Richie Clark," said Tim.

"Who's Richie Clark?" Ted asked.

"The biggest whiner in the division."

"Wouldn't you know he'd be the first to be last," Hambone said.

Ted looked around. Two of the brawnier Horsemen were holding down this little fat kid, whose tear-stained face was as pink as any piglet's. He writhed on the ground, screaming.

Jack stood over him. "Come on, Richie. Fair is fair. You *were* last."

"Noooooo," Richie wailed. "You can't make me."

Jack and the two Horsemen picked Richie up and carried him, kicking and screaming, to the trough. Without ceremony, they dumped him in.

At this point someone started laughing. A moment later everyone was. There was something ridiculously funny about Richie Clark, obviously a horrible kid, thrashing about in the watering trough. There was also more than a little relief among those who had saved their own skins. And somehow, because of the laughter, no one seemed to object to the rule anymore.

Ted turned to Lee. "You were almost right about my going in the trough."

"They'll never get you," Lee said. "You're too fast."

"You're no slouch yourself."

"No. I guess it's a good thing."

Lee smiled. Ted smiled back, then looked away. There

34

was Lee being nice to him again. But he'd behaved so badly and was obviously such a loser! Ted didn't want him to feel he wanted to be friends.

He turned to Hambone. "I don't understand. Why do we have to do something like this?"

Hambone held up his hands, palms up, the living embodiment of "How should I know?" "Beats me," he said. "But everyone goes on doing it, whatever it is, summer after summer. We must like testing ourselves, I guess. Trying to be macho guys. That's what this stuff is about. That and some of the all-American scouting tradition Jack was talking about. And you ain't seen nothin' yet!"

Ted wasn't so happy about that. In the cool mountain air, with the perspiration drying on his shirt, he felt chilled. "Kids at other camps don't do this," he said.

"Hell, no!" said Hambone. "That's the whole point. That's why guys keep coming back here. They don't like the soft life at those other camps."

"But what about Jack? What gives him the right to make the rules?"

Hambone shrugged again. "Jack's just one of those people. Style. Charisma. Magic. Call it what you want. Who knows how he got that way, but Higg thinks he's great, Mr. Bruce thinks he's great, everyone else just goes along, and Jack walks around doing what he wants."

Higg's voice, raised to a shout, overwhelmed them. "Everybody get your horses!"

Hambone slapped Ted on the back and gave him the thumbs-up sign. "Hey, man! Don't worry. You'll be fine. I can tell. Gotta go find Jim and Jake."

Later, while Ted was still searching the pasture for Nelly,

he ran into Jack. He was startled and embarrassed because he'd been talking about him such a short time ago, but he still couldn't get the damn watering-trough run out of his mind. He said, "I still don't get it. Why the rule?"

Jack snorted. A smile played around his mouth. "Surprised you, huh? You've got to understand this place. They want this kind of stuff. You may not think so, and everyone bitches and moans at first, but they really do. It's what Bruce wants, and, down deep, it's what Higg wants too. It's part of the Cherokee tradition."

"It doesn't seem necessary."

Jack poked him on the shoulder. "Come on, kid. You don't have any problems. Hey, there's Big Red. Catch you later."

But that wasn't the issue, Ted thought, standing alone now and looking out for Nelly. That wasn't the issue at all.

Nelly was hard to find. He tramped all over the pasture in the chill mist, dodging piles of manure, looking around clumps of trees, wondering all the while about Cherokee tradition and whether it felt good to be one of Jack's chosen few. Other Horsemen kept passing him by, leading their horses in by halter rope. Lee found Flash and hugged him. Just about everyone had gone in, and he was all the way at the other end of the pasture when there she was, glaring at him from behind a bush. Some ridiculous horse. Some Nelly.

She was trim and not very large. She had a beautiful bay coat, lovely brown eyes, and a well-proportioned head. He loved her at once, but when he went to offer his hand, she promptly shied away. He let her graze for a while, finding

36

himself amused at the way she steadfastly ignored him from a distance of fifteen feet. Then he walked up to her, and again she shied.

The game was becoming foolish. He let her calm down and begin to graze. Then he strode over, grabbed her halter, and attached his rope. She looked up at him as if this were the most surprising thing that had ever happened.

After feeding and grooming, everyone met in the upper barn, which was also the hayloft, to plan schedules. For the benefit of newcomers, Higg explained that the Horsemen would bring the horses up to the riding field after breakfast and ride from nine to ten. Then everyone would have an individual activity, but from eleven to twelve the entire division would have waterfront. This was a real pain in the ass because it meant rushing back from your activity, changing into bathing suits, and rushing the half mile to the lake, only to have to rush back at noon and bring the horses down before lunch, thereby defeating the purpose of the waterfront and getting sweaty and dirty all over again. Still, that's the way it was, and there was nothing they could do about it (a familiar approach by now, thought Ted). In the afternoon there would be group activities like baseball games and Capture-the-Flag and, of course, their usual Horsemen responsibilities. Evenings would be free form, depending on what came up.

The group sat on the floor as Higg walked up and down, filling in the details. It was as if he'd lost everyone to Jack in the early morning and was getting them all back now.

Ted chose riflery as his individual activity for the first half of the summer. So did Lee. Hambone and Tim were going to take Indian lore. When everyone had chosen, they all ran up the hill for breakfast.

37

And so it went that first week. The first time Ted mounted Nelly, she bolted. Even after he calmed her down, it was all he could do to keep her from flying out of the ring on some strange quest of her own. But after a few days she seemed less excitable, and, by the end of the week, even a little less headshy. Unexpected gestures could still be disastrous, producing snapped ropes and broken posts, but he was learning to be careful and teaching others to be as well.

Then there was riflery. He had advanced to Sharpshooter, Third Bar, in one week and was going for more. At the waterfront he was taking lifesaving, and in the first intra-camp baseball game, which was played over on the diamond behind the mess hall, the Horsemen beat the Seniors, 4–2. He'd played first base, had two hits (to go with Hambone's two), and Tim had pitched terrifically well.

Lee hadn't played in the game. He sat on the sidelines, but no one ever chose him to come in. His face got sadder and sadder, but he never said anything.

The rest of the time he was just friendly and sort of withdrawn. Every day he made sure Ted was out of bed, and sometimes in the mess hall or over at riflery, he'd try to say something nice. But Ted was keeping his distance, and somehow Lee knew not to press his luck.

Meanwhile, Ted was getting more of a kick out of Jack Dunn. Twice during the week, he made late-night visits to the clearing in the woods with Hambone and Tim, and Jack was always clever and outrageous. Tim went on playing it cool and hostile, but Jack could be counted on for anything. And it wasn't just beer and grass. He was even around at the daily after-breakfast inspections, making sure Higg didn't check too closely for dust under the beds.

There wasn't another incident until Thursday. Higg had just posted the list for an experimental polo team. Ted was on it, of course, despite a headshy Nelly. So were Hambone and Tim. Lee was not.

It was after supper. They'd just put the horses out to pasture. Ted was cleaning up Nelly's stall when he heard the yell. He rushed into the courtyard.

Lee was waving the list over his head. Ted tried to grab him. Lee pulled away.

"Hey," Ted said. "Stop it."

"Stop it?" said Lee. "Have you seen this list? Have you seen who's on it?"

"Yes," said Ted. "I have."

"Well, why wasn't I chosen then? I'm a better rider than half these guys."

"I don't know," said Ted. "It's Higg's list."

"Higg's list. Higg's list. Higg wouldn't choose me for anything. I never did anything to him. He just goes along with Jack."

"Lee, we've talked about this before."

"Doesn't matter. Doesn't matter what I do."

Higg appeared. "Is something wrong?"

Lee turned on him. "Why wasn't I chosen for this team?"

Higg removed the pipe from his mouth. "You weren't chosen because I didn't choose you."

Lee looked as if he'd been struck.

Higg put the pipe back in his mouth. He gave Ted a half smile and a half nod, as if to indicate there was just no reasoning with such people. Then he walked off.

Ted didn't know what to say. He just stood there, feeling like a fool.

The next day things got worse. They'd brought the horses down at dusk. It was hot, and everyone was sweaty and overtired. So when the run began up the hill, there was a lot of elbowing and shoving. Ted ran by Tim, who seemed to be keeping an even pace with Lee and a tall, thin kid called Mike Schroeder. Suddenly there was a shout. Lee was on the ground, and everyone was barreling past him.

There was no time to figure out what had happened. If you didn't get to the trough, you'd end up in it. When Ted was able to stop and look around, he saw Lee walking up the hill, holding a badly scraped left arm.

"Someone tripped me," he said.

"You fell," said Jack. "You go in."

"It's not fair," said Lee.

"Rules are rules," said Jack. "You were last."

"No!" said Lee.

Three other Horsemen went to help Jack. The four of them dumped Lee in the trough.

Lee sputtered and coughed. He looked as if he were about to cry. He stood up, soaking wet, and shouted, "You bastard, Jack Dunn! You fucking evil bastard!"

"Bastard, am I?" said Jack. "Evil, am I?"

He knocked Lee down. Then he pushed him under.

Ted was horrified. All the goodwill and good humor he'd felt toward Jack during the week vanished. This wasn't just a nasty rule. This was really vicious! He looked over at Jack, dark and strutting in front of the watering trough. He wanted to push him in, push him under, the way he'd pushed Lee.

But then he looked beyond Jack to Lee, sitting there so wet and defeated in the water. His thin black hair hung in strips over his forehead. His face had collapsed into narrow

40

planes. He could be such a good kid, but he was so easy to dislike. Why couldn't he understand about this kind of stuff? If he'd been a better sport about falling, if he'd just gone in and gotten wet, none of this would have happened. It was a hot day anyway. The water couldn't have been so bad. Why did he have to make such a big deal?

Riddled with mixed feelings, Ted went back to get washed for lunch. Lee caught up with him as he reached the mess hall.

"Why didn't you help me against Jack?"

Ted wondered himself, then looked again at this kid screaming at him. "I thought you were overreacting."

"I guess I can't expect much support from you!"

Ted swallowed hard. Did he really mean what he was about to say? "I've got nothing against being friends."

"Thanks," said Lee. "Thanks a lot."

And he walked off.

Six

A half mile downhill through the woods, the dirt road to Cherokee Lake was covered in shade. Because it was so cool going down, campers no longer felt hot and sweaty and eager for a swim by the time they reached the water. Because the incline was steep going up, by the time they reached the camp they felt cranky and winded and no longer refreshed from the dip.

At six-thirty in the morning, though, none of this mattered. It was just freezing cold, so cold Ted couldn't imagine why anyone would want to be in the vicinity, much less wandering around in a bathrobe and moccasins carrying soap and a towel. But it was Saturday morning and time for the Saturday morning dip, and that's exactly what he was doing.

No one had had to wake him. Everyone in camp participated in this little maneuver, and promptly at six-thirty reveille had blasted out of the public-address system. Ted was so unaccustomed to waking up to a bugle call, he'd shot a foot in the air.

Shouldn't we get to sleep late on weekends? was his first thought. It didn't linger long.

"Okay, babies!" Doug shouted. "I don't like this any better

than you do, but start getting it together. The sooner we get down there, the sooner we get back."

"Yeah," said Ted. "It'll toughen us up."

Everyone laughed except Lee.

"Can't wait to be so tough, my skin turns to parchment," said Hambone, beating on his chest.

"Is that when they make you a mummy?" said Tim.

"No," said Hambone, "a daddy."

Even Lee laughed this time. "Maybe," Ted said, "what we really need around here are some girls."

"Never happen," said Doug. "Old man Bruce couldn't have his traditional skinny dip if there were girls."

"Oh, I don't know," Ted said, "there might be a better reason for it then."

"Yeah," said Hambone. "Good idea. Next year coed!"

"Okay, guys," said Doug, belting his robe around his paunch. "Get your tails out that door."

And now here they were, tramping down the road, trying to stay warm, as more and more robed figures emerged and joined them. It was like a procession of ghosts through a forest gray with dawn.

Ted noticed Lee was walking on the other side of the road and hoped he hadn't alienated him completely. He wound his towel around his neck. The air was so cold, he could see his breath.

"Hey, Hambone," he said over his shoulder, "what is so terrific about going swimming at six A.M.?"

"Nothing I know of, babe," said Hambone. "Maybe it'll make us better men."

Ted laughed.

"But I thought we were here to be riding and learning about horses."

"We are, we are, but the one just goes along with the other. It's like I told you before. What's here is here, and people can't hate it too much, or they wouldn't keep coming back."

"But the wrong thing seems to have become the important thing."

"Hey, come on now, Ted. That's enough 'buts' for one day. If I didn't think you were such a good guy, I'd want to punch you out. I may not like this dip very much, but I'll damn well go down there and dive in with the best of 'em!"

Hambone grabbed Tim around the shoulders. Immediately they began walking like zombies, feet dragging, singing "Seven more weeks of vacation, then we go to the station, back to ci-vi-li-za-tion, *I wanna go home!*"

There was nothing else to do. Ted joined in on the next chorus. Then Doug said, "All right, you guys, knock it off. It's too early in the morning."

They all gave him the raspberry. But they shut up, too, until they reached the lake, where, as they had anticipated, a pale gray sky hung over the still water.

Little ripples formed around the pilings of the dock. There was the pock-pock sound of bobbing canoes. It all looked and felt very cold.

They sat in rows on the grass, elbows around knees for warmth. Why wasn't Jack here? Oh yes, there he was, over on the edge of the group, his favorite position.

When everyone had arrived, T. R. Bruce walked matter-of-factly to the middle of the dock. He stripped himself of his robe and pajamas and plunged in, a lean, gray body disturbing dark green water. He made a "brrrr" sound and splashed about, soaping up, making little eddies of soap all around him. When he was through, he ducked under and jumped in the air. "Okay. Everybody in!"

No one budged.

"All right, you guys," Doug Parelli barked. "Get your butts into that water."

"Since when have you been such a sport?" said Hambone.

"None of your lip," said Doug. "Just get going."

"After you," said Ted.

"I'm going, Jenner. Just have to make sure all you bull-shitters don't run out on me."

"Us?" said Tim. "Never."

"Okay, Seniors," said one of their counselors, "all together."

The Seniors stood. In a group, they moved toward the water.

Doug was beside himself. "Are you guys going to let those Seniors beat you out? I thought you were Horsemen. You're nothing but a bunch of pansies!"

Hambone ripped off his robe, ran down the bank, and dove into the water. He made a huge splash and came up gasping. "Eeeeeeeaaaahhhhh!" he yelled, and all the Horsemen followed him in, scattering Seniors right and left.

In minutes the shallow area, crowded with scrubbing campers and counselors, was filled with soap suds. As they finished, some kids dove under the floats and lines and began swimming for the raft.

Ted scrubbed up and rinsed off as fast as he could. The water was so cold you never quite warmed up in it, and not wearing a bathing suit made things worse. Even so, it was warmer in the water than in the frozen air, so he tried to keep everything but his head under as much as he could. This made it difficult to go on soaping, but he figured the whole thing was pretty much of an empty gesture anyway and didn't worry about it. He didn't move around too much. The water was so full of people—Hambone was floundering nearby, and Lee was scrubbing frantically—there was always the danger of being kicked or elbowed in a delicate place.

Swimming to the raft was out of the question. His only interest was in getting out of the water as quickly as possible without calling attention to himself. As a few Intermediates and Seniors straggled out, Ted drifted after them. He had reached his towel, dried himself vigorously to stop the shivering, and was putting on his robe when the shout went up.

Halfway to the raft, a boy was struggling. His head bobbed up and went under. His arms lifted and disappeared.

Jack Dunn had just climbed out on the dock. He dove back in and swam to the boy, then got him turned around and into a cross-chest carry. As he dragged him out onto the bank, a cheer went up. But Jack paid no attention. He checked the boy over and made sure artificial respiration wasn't necessary.

It wasn't. The boy sat up and seemed fine. But before Jack could get his robe on, T. R. Bruce put an arm around his shoulders. Most of the campers and counselors were out of the water now, and Mr. Bruce addressed them.

"We should all be grateful to Jack Dunn," he said. " No

one else was there to rescue Mark Milton, and he was not only there but equal to the task. I think we owe Jack a round of applause to go with that cheer."

Everyone whistled and clapped. Jack smiled broadly at Mr. Bruce, who looked as if he were presenting an award. Ted clapped along with the rest, but he felt really weird about it. He couldn't join his image of Jack Dunn pushing Lee down in the watering trough with this image of Jack Dunn the rescuer, Jack Dunn the hero. Which was the real Jack, or were they both real? Still, warm now in his robe and towel, he had to be just a little proud of being part of Jack Dunn's inner circle.

Back at the cabin, with the sun starting to emerge, it was time to choose jobs for Director's Inspection. Hambone volunteered to straighten clothes and shine shoes. Lee said he'd police the area.

"Okay," said Doug, "but who's going to be sweeper? You know it's no worse than anything else."

"Yeah," said Hambone, "'cause you don't have to do it."

"All that stuff to move," said Lee. "All those shoes."

"True, true," said Doug, "but each of you is going to do it sometime. I'm also aware that the only people speaking are the ones who have already volunteered. How about it, babes? Which of you will it be?"

Ted realized he could wipe away the memory of his conversation with Hambone on the road by making an extra effort now.

"I'll do it," he said. "I don't mind."

"Whoopeee!" said Hambone.

"Now wait a minute," said Tim. "I do the best job."

"Sorry, Timmy," said Doug. "Too little too late. How about arranging mess kits on beds and straightening trunks? You can do the sweeping next time."

Tim gave Ted such a dirty look, it was almost a sneer. Then he shot up the ladder to make his bed.

Everyone got down to work. And when they were finished with making their beds and doing their jobs, they got to work on themselves. Finger and toenails had to be clipped and cleaned. Hair had to be combed. Ears were cleaned, and teeth brushed.

When T. R. Bruce, in khaki shirt and khaki pants, and Nurse Sims, in her uniform, came by, four clean boys lined up in their underwear. They extended their hands, palm down.

Mr. Bruce passed down the line, examining posture, finger and toenails, and overall appearance. Nurse Sims followed, looking for cuts, bruises, anything that might require a few swabs of Merthiolate or worse.

"Shall we go inside?" said Mr. Bruce.

"All yours," said Doug Parelli.

Inside was the picture of neat. Neat trunks (all items folded in rows). Neat clothes rack (all hangers facing the same way). Neat shoes (all polished in rows beside the beds). Neat beds (the quarter bounced on each). Neat mess kits (pan, pot, cup, and silverware clean and lined up on each bed). Neat floor.

"Well, well," said T. R. Bruce, kneeling under Doug's bed, "someone's actually done a good job of sweeping."

"It was Jenner," said Doug. "He does a good job."

Mr. Bruce looked at Ted. "I've been hearing good things

about you from other people, too. It's nice to know you're consistent."

Other people, too? "Thank you, sir," said Ted.

"Now what about the outside area?"

Everyone trooped outside with Mr. Bruce and followed him as he patrolled the grass around the cabin. He'd gone down one side and was just reaching the rear when Ted noticed a crumpled candy wrapper beside a cinderblock support. Quickly he motioned to Lee. Just as quickly he said, "Mr. Bruce, did you ever notice these blue flowers back here? They seem to be everywhere."

Mr. Bruce looked where Ted was pointing. "Why yes," he said, "those are cornflowers, Jenner. Are you a botanist as well, to go with your other talents?"

"No, sir," said Ted. "I just thought they were pretty."

And that was it. No points lost on the outside. No points lost on the inside, unless Mr. Bruce wasn't telling. No points lost for personal hygiene. The boys hugged each other as T. R. Bruce and Nurse Sims departed for Cabin 2. They had to have a perfect score!

"Now into some clothes," said Doug. "And Fischer, have you ever thought about glasses?"

"It was just a mistake," said Lee. "I'm sorry."

"It's okay," said Doug. "Just remember for next time."

At breakfast, when the results of Director's Inspection were finally announced, Cabin 3 had won the Horseman Division with a perfect score of ten. They would all get seconds on ice cream at Sunday lunch.

Hambone poked Ted in the ribs. "We couldn't have done it without you, kid!"

Ted was really pleased. He'd joined in and made a contribution.

"Hooray for us," said Tim, in a low voice dripping with sarcasm.

"Nice going, all of you," said Doug.

Lee didn't say anything to anyone.

Seven

For the Horsemen of Camp Cherokee, Sunday afternoon meant tack cleaning. Saturday night there had been a campfire back at the Indian ceremonial grounds off the road to the lake with lots of marshmallows for toasting and endless choruses of those old camp favorites, "I've Been Working on the Railroad" and "The Moonshiner Song." This morning everyone had gone back to that same circle for a nonsectarian chapel service devoted to the greatness of God and country and good fellowship, culminating in the hymn "Our God, Our Help in Ages Past." Now, full of the tepid roast chicken, powdered mashed potatoes, and frozen carrots and peas of Sunday lunch, and having enjoyed a nap during rest hour, most of the camp had free play while the Horsemen worked.

Ted didn't mind at all. He'd hung Nelly's saddle over the side of her stall and was busy rubbing a sponge thick with saddle soap into the skirts and flaps. When he finished those, he would get to the pommel and seat, and after that he'd turn the saddle over and reach all those underparts where sweat collected. Every so often, he dipped his sponge into a bucket of water and wrung it dry before rubbing it in the soap and developing a rich lather.

Higg had shown him how to do this before he started,

had explained that if you left your sponge too wet, the lather would be all watery and you'd end up drying out the leather instead of preserving it. They'd been simple instructions, but they'd come from so much love of horses and their care, Ted had been moved. So now, as he worked the soap into the leather and around the buckles and rings, he felt as if he were really accomplishing something, as if all this work on a beautiful sunny afternoon had some kind of meaning in relation to himself and Nelly and Higg and the other Horsemen—as if, somehow, with all of them working this way, there was something binding them together.

He was also thinking about Jack Dunn and how, last night at the campfire, with the flames crackling and all their faces glowing red, he had sung the loudest chorus of "The Moonshiner Song." How fitting that had seemed. How well that chorus seemed to define Jack's attitude toward the world.

The words echoed in Ted's ears:

> I'm a rambler, I'm a gambler
> I'm a long way from home
> And if you don't like me
> Just leave me alone
> I'll eat when I'm hungry
> I'll drink when I'm dry
> And if moonshine don't kill me
> I'll live till I die.

Jack just did what he wanted. Isn't that what Hambone had said? Sometimes it came out good and sometimes not so good, but whatever it was, he didn't mind the risk. And if you didn't like him, he couldn't have cared less. But if he didn't like *you*. . . . No, it didn't make sense. Lee was laying too much blame on Jack for everything.

Ted went on soaping. Already his saddle was beginning to shine. Across the yard, Jack had slung Big Red's saddle over the pasture fence. Hambone, Tim, Jack's brother Ricky, and a couple of other guys had brought theirs over, too. They were all busy soaping and shooting the breeze. Every so often, a burst of laughter would go up as someone told another awful joke.

Ted could have been with them. But with the horses out to pasture for the day, he was enjoying these moments by himself, enjoying standing in Nelly's stall and working at his own speed. He had just finished with the saddle and was starting to rub the bits of dried grass off the corners of Nelly's snaffle bit when he heard, "Hey, Ted, why don't you join us?"

It was Jack, of course, waving him over to the fence.

"What's the matter? You a stranger or something?"

Ted chuckled to himself. There went all his intentions of being alone. "Okay," he said. "Coming."

Reluctantly Ted picked up Nelly's bridle and carried it over. Well, not so reluctantly at that.

"That's more like it," said Jack, patting him on the back. "Don't want you getting lonely on us now."

Ted nodded. "Thought I could do without you. Guess I was wrong."

He dumped Nelly's bridle over a fencepost and began soaping it. He'd done the cheek straps and the brow band when Jack wandered over.

"Got something going tomorrow night."

"Oh, really?"

"Interested?"

Ted had no idea what Jack meant. "Sure," he said. "What is it?"

"Won't tell you now. Meet us by the mess hall after lights out."

"Who's us?"

"What are all these questions? You coming or not?"

Ted juggled the sponge in his hands. It was as if he were under a spell. The spell made him both happy and unhappy, but there it was. "Of course I'm coming. What do you think?"

After dinner Monday, Mr. Bruce announced that tonight would be the first haunted-house trip of the season. He had chosen the first three Intermediate cabins to go. They would meet on the porch of the administration building after lights out. They would drive into town for a special snack and then pay a visit to the Wilson house, where they'd be able to show their bravery. After that, they would sleep out overnight and return to camp for breakfast in the morning.

All of this was said so matter-of-factly no one had any reaction. Suddenly Ted realized that this was the first of those trips Lee had mentioned on the train. He looked across the table. Lee was glaring at him.

Whatever Jack had going for tonight, it had to involve the trip. And whatever Jack had arranged, it now included Ted Jenner.

The night was dark and overcast, with an eerie kind of quiet. As Ted lay in bed, listening to the mournful sound of taps—"Day is done, gone the sun"—roll out over the camp, he couldn't help but feel scared for those three bunks of Intermediate kids gathering their flashlights and their extra sweaters. He also had to wonder just what Jack was going to be up to and whether it would be more of that stuff he'd said everyone really wanted.

A moment after taps, the lights winked out in all the cabins. Doug Parelli switched off the lights in Cabin 3. "Good night, sweet princes. Hope all your dreams are wet ones."

"Ha, ha," said Tim from bed. And Lee echoed, "Ha, ha."

"Thank you, thank you," said Doug. And he took a little bow before scooting out the door.

Ted wondered who would be joining Jack at the mess hall. Hambone had gone off to Crescent Lake with two bunks of Junior boys. Would it be Mike Schroeder or Ricky Dunn? He hoped it wouldn't be Ricky. Jack's younger brother was the same tall, loose-limbed package as Jack, but he had a kind of insolence about him Ted didn't like. He heard two feet thump gently to the floor and some carefully muffled footsteps, and he knew who one of his comrades was going to be.

He waited until Tim was safely out the door. Then he hurried into his clothes.

"Have a good time," came the voice.

Ted stopped. "Lee, I don't want you to misunderstand—"

"What's to misunderstand?"

"Jack asked me to meet him."

"Obviously. You're becoming one of his flunkies."

"That's not true. We're . . . friends."

"No one becomes friends with Jack Dunn. So now you're going to help haunt houses."

"I don't know what we'll be doing."

"That's smart. What else would Jack be doing tonight?"

"You'd just like to be coming along."

"No, I don't think so."

"Well, so long then."

"I think you'll be sorry."

Sneaking across the field to the mess hall, Ted was furious at Lee. First for making him feel like a fool. Second for making Jack seem like a louse when nothing had even happened yet. He was just embarrassed about missing that candy wrapper at Director's Inspection. And mad about being left out again.

Jack was waiting in the shadows. So were Tim and Ricky. Well, if nothing else, Ted had made some right guesses. They watched the Intermediate campers—very small, very frightened—drive off with Mr. Bruce in the GMC. Then Jack waved them over to the camp ranchwagon.

Tim and Ted got in the back seat. Jack and Ricky sat up front. Jack drove.

His driving was wild and erratic. They careened around corners and shot past stop signs. Jack had never heard of speed limits, it seemed, or road courtesy. He crowded cars over as he passed, swerved in front of them as he pulled ahead, and all the while he was turning around and gesturing with his hands, laughing and talking.

"Oh, boy," he said. "I can't wait to scare the shit out of those little kids. Can't you just see their faces!"

"First time out," said Ricky. "We'd better be good."

Jack screeched around a curve on the wrong side of the road. He just missed plowing into a tree.

"Oh, we'll be good. And Ted is going to make us even better. Right, Ted?"

Ted was hanging onto the strap by the window. No one had explained, but no one needed to. "Right, Jack," he said. "You got it."

But what could he be right about? What could they possibly be doing? Tim was staring out the window. He wasn't going to be any help. And what about Jack? There was an edge to him now, something closer to the way he'd been with Lee at the watering trough and at the clearing in the woods that first night. Wait a minute. Jack was a hero. Not many campers got chosen to help haunt houses. Better wise up and go with it.

A car swerved around them. The driver angrily honked his horn.

"Whoopeee!" Jack shouted. "Same to you, buddy. Next time I'll run you off the road!"

"Oh, great!" said Ted. But he laughed in spite of himself.

"Glad to hear you laughing," said Jack.

"Let's hope some cop doesn't hear me."

"Yeah. We might have to bail you out of jail."

The ranchwagon slowed imperceptibly, then bounced off the hardtop onto a heavily rutted dirt road. There was a spray of pebbles and dust. The wagon shuddered and burst forward as Jack struggled to control the wheel.

He slowed down, and they continued uphill, twisting and bouncing and straining to see in the almost total blackness. Trees lined either side of the road. Only as they reached the top of the hill and turned left into a grove that hid them completely did Ted catch a glimpse, off on the right, of an old house.

Slamming car doors sounded like thunder claps. Jack locked up, and the four of them crossed the road, found the path between the trees, and made their way through deep grass and up a little rise to the house.

It was tall and gaunt—a front porch, two floors, and an attic slumped slightly over to the left. The shed out back had fallen in, most of the windows were broken, and paint had all but disappeared from the rotting timbers. In daylight the whole effect might have been relatively harmless, but at night what you got was menace.

Arched against the night sky, the house was a black hulk glowering from sightless eyes. It also smelled disgusting, as if a hundred bums had lived there for years.

Who could possibly want to go near this place? thought Ted as he climbed the porch steps, opened the front door (which creaked, of course), and got a stronger whiff of that terrible smell. It had been bad enough climbing the rise and feeling the chill settle over him like cold rain. Now, though he knew perfectly well that the only people here were the four of them, he was struck by the absolute certainty that they were not alone. Had Jack not grabbed his arm and ushered him inside, he might have run.

Well, maybe not. Still, he wouldn't want to be here all alone, not knowing what to expect. The kids coming here tonight were only twelve years old!

The front room had nothing in it but an old rocking chair. That seemed pretty harmless, but Jack was pointing up the stairs.

He followed Ricky and Tim. The banister was half gone,

and some of the boards were rotten. Ted pressed his hand against the wall to keep his balance.

When he reached the top, Ricky said, "Is the stuff here?"

The question echoed in the darkness. "Sure," said Jack. "Right where we left it. No one's been here since last summer."

Somehow that response seemed vaguely reassuring, though just what the "stuff" was remained a mystery for the moment. Ted hoped that mystery wouldn't last too long.

Climbing onto the landing himself, he clicked on his flashlight. The light was comforting, too, but what he saw was weird. For some reason the landing was not just a landing but a bedroom. There was a double bed covered with some sort of dusty quilt and a battered end table with a lamp on it. Two bedrooms were off to the right, but they had nothing in them at all.

"Jack," said Ted, "explain."

"Nothing to it," said Jack. "A kid comes to the house, knocks on the door, and runs away for a B, or he comes up these stairs and shines a light out the front window for a B+. He can go around the house for a B+, too, but for some reason the really brave suckers all want to come inside. When the kid comes up the stairs, it's easier to scare him on the landing than in a bedroom. Then he can run back down the stairs. In the bedrooms they start to panic. Unless, of course, they don't get scared on the landing. Then they probably won't get scared in the bedrooms anyway."

All that sounded pretty reasonable. "And the stuff?"

"Oh, Ricky and I have a few things we use on the landing. You and Tim, each of you gets a bedroom. There are piles of rocks by the windows. Throw 'em out, make some noise.

When a kid comes in, scare him away. You know. Make something up. We've also got a string that rocks the rocking chair."

Jack seemed distracted, almost drunk on the idea of what was about to happen.

Ted asked, "How long does this go on?"

"Depends on the number of brave ones. Shouldn't be many tonight."

He waved Ted into the front bedroom and Tim into the side one. "Jenner," he said, "you're the lookout. When a kid comes up that path, you let us know. Okay, places!"

Jack's use of that word made it all seem like a crazy play. As Ted went into the front bedroom, he wished he knew the ending.

This empty, dark room was scarier than a room full of furniture would have been. He'd been glad Tim and his smirking face had been stuck somewhere else. Now he almost wished Tim were there.

Some crumpled old newspapers lay on the floor. He turned his flashlight beam on one. It was too water stained to read, but the date was 1936. Someone had brought these papers into the house. And again he felt that eerie presence, as if that someone were still there.

Ted kicked at the pile of rocks and opened the window a crack. Cold air poured through. Despite the dark, from where he stood he had a perfect view of the path below. Jack was right. He was the ideal lookout. And any kid coming up those stairs was heading for this room!

Second thoughts. Ted's "Sure, why nots" were getting overrun by a voice that said, "Why the hell are you doing this?" Then it no longer mattered how he felt. The GMC, headlights blazing, came up the hill.

"Flashlights out!" Jack barked.

They were in darkness. Jack and Ricky crouched on the other side of the bed.

Ted watched the GMC pull over a good way down from the house. He saw the headlights wink out and heard the kids' voices as they emerged. Mr. Bruce's voice was a louder whisper than the rest, always reassuring, always calm.

Dark figures moved up the road beyond the trees, then turned right onto the path. They huddled together. There were more whisperings and some obvious explaining by Mr. Bruce, then a few nervous laughs and a volunteer.

The boy started up the path to the house. The grass was so high, you could hardly see his head. He'd made it about halfway when Ted dropped two rocks out the window and grunted loudly. The boy stopped in his tracks. His mouth dropped open. He turned and ran.

"Well," T. R. Bruce whispered, "that's not so good, Williams. I have to give you a double X. In fact, you're lucky it's not an XXX + !"

There were muted protests. "I'm sorry," said Mr. Bruce. "Who's next?"

After a moment's pause, as the boys assessed their chances and their fear, another victim started up the path.

When he was a little more than halfway, Ted dropped a rock and laughed a deep, mocking laugh. Around the side, he heard Tim do the same.

Again, the boy stopped—and listened. Then he started running toward the house!

"This kid's coming!" Ted whispered. "And he's coming fast!"

"We're ready," said Jack.

The kid pounded on the door. "Hello, Mr. Wilson?" he

said so quickly the words were slurred. "Can we camp here for the night?"

Then he raced down the path again.

How weird, Ted thought. Bruce is telling them that the ghosts of the Wilsons are still in the house. Given the way he felt himself, that wasn't so hard to believe.

"Not bad, Henson," he heard Mr. Bruce say. "You got your B."

Ted shifted from one foot to the other in the darkness. He zipped his parka up to the neck. Another boy started toward the house.

This time Ted dropped a whole shower of rocks out the window. The boy stopped, then kept on coming. Ted laughed his laugh and pretended he was gagging. The boy mounted the porch steps.

"I think we've got a live one," Ted said.

"Gotcha," said Jack.

The boy opened the front door. He stepped inside. The rocking chair began rocking slowly back and forth with no one in it. The boy watched this for a moment, then started up the stairs.

Each stair creaked as he stepped on it. As he reached the landing, Jack whispered, "Go." He and Ricky flew over the bed. Jack tackled the boy—short and redheaded—and held him down. Ricky slipped a potato sack over his head.

The boy squirmed. "No," he gasped.

When Ricky had the sack as far as the waist, Jack jumped up. The two of them forced the body the rest of the way in. The boy kept squirming and protesting, but Jack held the sack closed at the top and none of it made any difference.

From his position at the window, Ted watched in disbelief. But what came next was worse.

Inside the sack, the boy began kicking and screaming.

"Stop it," Jack hissed, "if you know what's good for you."

The sack went limp and quiet. Ricky tied it with twine. Jack threw it on the bed. Then he half threw it at Ricky.

Ricky dropped it. It landed on the floor with a bump. The screams began again, screams that were more terrible for coming from this bloblike figure in a potato sack.

"I told you once to stop it," Jack growled. "I won't tell you again."

He kicked the sack. Ricky kicked it, too. The screams turned to sobs. The sack began to tremble.

"Shut up," Jack said.

"Shut up," Ricky said.

Each of them kicked the sack again.

At that moment another boy reached the top of the stairs. Ted hadn't seen him arrive. Numb with shock, he'd both forgotten about the window and done nothing to stop Jack and Ricky.

The boy caught a glimpse of what was happening. He shrieked. Jack dove for him, but he was already halfway down the stairs. Jack picked himself up and lunged. But the kid was out the door and running down the path. His shrieks were so loud, they could be heard for miles.

Hearing him, seeing him come flying in their direction, the other kids panicked.

"Wait," Mr. Bruce said, "nothing has happened."

But that wasn't good enough. As a group, the boys ran for the car. There was a ferocious slamming of doors as they piled inside.

Jack and Ricky watched all this from Ted's window. "I guess that's it," Jack said.

"Yup," said Ricky.

"Better open the sack," said Jack.

Dazed and bruised, the redheaded boy was pulled to his feet.

"Okay, kid," Jack said. "Fun's over. Remember—not a word about who was here."

He looked the boy in the eye. "Right?"

The boy looked back, terrified. "Right."

"Okay now. Go."

The boy took off. Ted watched him streak down the path and catch the GMC as the headlights flashed on.

Jack and Ricky came back into the bedroom. At that moment Tim appeared.

"Well," said Jack, and he laughed. "I guess you might say we've had a full night's work."

"How about a beer?" said Tim.

"Yeah," said Jack. "How about a beer?"

Eight

The dark trees slid by on either side of the road. The sliver of sky between them was only a little less dark. Ted leaned back as far as he could in his seat. He pressed his cheek against the cold window pane.

Jack was careening back and forth. He'd pulled out a six-pack of Bud and was waving a can around. "Hey, Ted, this is for you," he said, turning, almost losing control of the wheel.

They'd decided to drink on the move. Didn't want to get in too late.

"No, thanks," said Ted.

"Okay," said Jack. "Your loss."

He handed beers to the others. No one seemed to have anything to say.

Jack drove on. He took a slug of beer. "Could you believe that redheaded kid? I never thought he'd be so tough."

"I never thought he'd be so heavy," said Ricky.

His face was suddenly illuminated by the lights of a passing car. Paler than Jack, with hair a lighter brown, he was smiling.

Jack laughed.

Ted said, "I don't understand."

"What's that?"

Ted's mouth refused to form the words. They lodged in his throat, like pebbles.

"Is something the matter?"

Jack was at his friendliest, his most seductive.

"Yes," Ted said. "There is."

"Well, why don't you just tell us. We're all friends here."

The car swerved around a corner, tires screeching. Ted held on. He looked across at Tim's smirking face. Hardly the face of a friend.

The road straightened out again. He said, "Why did you have to beat the kid? And the sack—"

"Hey, come on," said Jack. "This is haunted-house stuff. Next time we'll let you do the sack."

"I don't think it's right. Beating the kid, kicking him—"

"It's all part of the fun.

"Beating someone up isn't fun."

"Don't be such a schmuck. Tomorrow that kid and the other one'll be swaggering around camp boasting about how brave they were. How one of them got captured and the other one almost did and how they both escaped. Everyone who hears the story will be scared to death. And they'll all want to go on the next haunted-house trip! One of the reasons kids keep coming back here is the haunted-house trips!"

"But there have to be limits. This is camp, not war. You went too far."

Jack was silent for a moment. Then he said, ever so casually, "Ted, it's a good thing I like you. So what if we went too far? Going too far is what it's all about. The kids like it when we get extra tough."

"Those kids were a little small for that. I wonder if Mr. Bruce would approve."

Jack smiled. "Don't you think we're here *because* Mr. Bruce approves? He may not know the details—and no one's ever going to tell him—but what we're doing fits right in with his whole tough-guy image of this place."

Ted wanted to say something smart in return, wanted to lean forward and thrust a fist into that smooth-talking, smiling face. But as he listened to Jack, he realized he was right. At this camp, no one would condemn these awful beatings. No one would even begin to tell Mr. Bruce about them because nothing they could say would seem so terrible. Besides, Mr. Bruce would take Jack's word, no matter what. No one at Camp Cherokee would have the guts to stand up against Jack Dunn.

Then Ted realized something else. He might still be in Jack's power, might continue to be lured into acceptance by Jack's presence and his words and—he had to admit it—by fear. But that power would not last forever. Jack was too extreme for that, and he would do something to push Ted over the edge. And when he did, afraid or not, Ted was going to have to act against him.

"Well," said Jack, "I assume you've been doing some good thinking about what I've said and have realized how right I am. Are you still with us?"

"Oh," said Ted, coming up for air. "Oh, sure."

Jack pounded on the wheel. "Good going, Ted. That's what I wanted to hear."

He turned sharply to the left. The car bounced up the Old Glory Road and stopped in front of the mess hall. They were back where they'd started.

During the next week, Ted became increasingly popular, and not just among the Horsemen.

The Horsemen liked him first because he was such a good rider (almost but not quite as good as Tim) and second because he was trying so hard—and actually beginning to succeed—with Nelly. They also liked him because he was easygoing and didn't complain. When it was time for barn detail, he hoisted his shovel and did barn detail. When it was time to run up the hill, he ran.

He'd also begun helping the little kids onto their horses before leaving the riding field in the mornings and afternoons. That got him acquainted with some of them, and they began saying "Hi, Ted" whenever he passed by. He always said "Hi" back, and one morning Chip Polk, a little Junior boy, came running up to him.

"Hi, Chip," said Ted, "how ya doin'?"

"Hi, Ted," said Chip, "I'm fine. I've got something for you."

He held out a paper bag.

Ted took it. Inside was a key ring Chip had made in arts and crafts.

"Hey, thanks, Chip," said Ted. "This is really great."

But Chip was so embarrassed he'd already dashed away.

Then there was the help Ted gave to other members of his lifesaving class when they couldn't follow Monty Benson's explanations and how he handled the choosing of the kids when he was asked to be captain of a team for Capture-the-Flag. All the campers were gathered in the middle of the riding field. Jim Burns, the opposing captain, stood on one side of them. Ted, wearing a frayed T-shirt and blue-jean cutoffs, stood on the other. Jim had first pick, and he chose a Senior. Then Ted chose a Horseman. Jim chose another Senior, and Ted chose an Intermediate! A little kid instead of an older kid! Then Jim chose a Horseman, and Ted chose another Intermediate! And Jim chose another Horseman, and Ted chose a Junior!

Things went on like this for a while, and everyone got really stirred up. It didn't make much difference—everyone finally got chosen anyway—but for the younger kids, so accustomed to being taken last, it was a real boost. In fact, they got so excited and pumped up, they won the game. Two Intermediate boys, Phil Beck and Ken Steinberg, raced into enemy territory, freed all the prisoners, and stole the flag in one neatly executed maneuver. They were so fast, no one laid a hand on them.

And so it went. Ted was becoming so involved in one thing and another—in riflery he was up to Sharpshooter, Fifth Bar, and gaining—he hardly had time to notice Lee. He'd see him at meals or in the cabin, but he never had much to say to him, and Lee seemed to have become guarded and more introspective than ever. Lee had been asleep when Ted had gotten back from the haunted-house trip, and neither one of them had brought up the subject, either the next day or any other day. Every so often Ted thought he saw Lee looking at him strangely, as if, somehow, he had abandoned him. Maybe he had. Lee was such an odd combination of things, he didn't know if he wanted the friendship or not.

He waved the thought away. As for Jack, he seemed to be trying extra hard to keep the spell working. Jokes on the way to flag-raising. Arm around the shoulder while waiting for canteen. Ted wasn't going down to the clearing in the woods much, but when he went, he was more than welcome.

Tim, on the other hand, continued to snub him at every opportunity. Finally it was too much.

Tim had shot ahead of him leaving the mess hall after dinner. He was passing the tennis courts when Ted caught up to him.

"I'd like to talk with you."

Tim whirled around. "You want to talk to me? Start talking!"

"You shouldn't be so threatened by me."

"Threatened? Why should I be threatened? I'm the best camper, and you're terrific. Everyone knows that."

"Tim, there's no reason we can't be friends."

Tim's forced smile spread over his round baby face. "But Ted, you don't understand. We *are* friends. We've always been friends. Now if you'll excuse me, I'd like to get back to the bunk before evening activity."

Ted watched him stride impatiently across the vast green lawn. The cause was obviously lost, and he felt badly. But at least he'd given it his best shot.

Nine

Saturday. At breakfast following Director's Inspection, Mr. Bruce announced that Camp Loraine, a girls' camp three miles away, had invited the older boys at Cherokee to a square dance. The problem was they had also invited boys from other camps in the area, so only a dozen Cherokee boys could go.

"Anyone on the list who wants to back out, please report to the administration building after breakfast," Mr. Bruce said. "We will be glad to make substitutions."

Mr. Bruce and Head Counselor Bud Wells had made the right choices. Ted, Jack, Ricky, Hambone, and Tim were on the list. So were Mike Schroeder, Jim Burns, and several eager Seniors. Not one of them would have preferred a Saturday night movie in camp to the prospect of meeting some girls.

"Girls!" said Jack as Bud Wells, blond and twinkly, pulled the GMC into the parking lot at Camp Loraine. "Lead me to 'em!"

Bud laughed. "Just hold on, Jack, and let me park the car first."

"I don't think I can stand it. It's been so long."

"Yeah," said Ricky. "About two weeks."

"I don't know," said Jack, clawing at an imaginary tie.

"I'm so desperate, my mind's a blank."

"Yeah, yeah," said Tim. "If you're that desperate, you should stay in the car and jerk off."

Ted cringed. The one thing he really missed at Camp Cherokee was having girls around. He wanted this to be a great evening and hoped it wouldn't be spoiled by these guys making fools of themselves.

As they walked from the parking lot up a hill to a large, wooden rec hall, Jack seemed to calm down and Ted relaxed. They were all dressed in sport shirts, clean jeans, and boots, ranging from cowboy to engineer. In fact, they all looked so good, it was hard to imagine that two hours earlier, half these guys had been knee-deep in horse manure and smelling like it, too.

Looking around, Ted was instantly aware of how different Camp Loraine was from Camp Cherokee. There were no rugged cabins arranged in perfect order around a semicircle. Here the bunks looked like little bungalows. They were white with red or blue trim, and they dotted the hillside in no particular order.

He liked the color and the randomness of it all. It seemed to indicate a kind of freedom and casualness, a willingness to be part of and at ease with the rest of the world, that would never be found at Camp Cherokee. Sure, this was more like a girls' than a boys' camp, but it also seemed a lot more like other camps he'd heard about from kids at home. Some of those camps were for boys, some for girls, and a lot of them were coed.

He was walking beside tall, lanky Mike Schroeder. "Hey, Mike," he said, "why do you think our camp isn't more like this one?"

"This one's for girls," said Mike.

"No, that's not what I mean. I know Loraine's for girls and stuff, but why couldn't Cherokee be—I don't know— a little more relaxed?"

"Because we don't want it to be. We like it the way it is."

"But don't you think it would be fun to have more contact with the outside world, go on field trips and things, maybe even have more dances like this one?"

"No. We like things the way they are. The horses are great, and the kids like to stick together. We can do all that other stuff at home. The only reason we go to this one dance is that someone here at Camp Loraine talked Mr. Bruce into it a long time ago and it's become a tradition."

Ted was speechless. He knew he shouldn't have been surprised to hear this, but he was. Mike went on.

"Besides, the parents like Cherokee the way it is too."

"They do?"

"Sure, I guess they like to know their kids are mostly in the same place with the same people leading a healthy, rugged life. Stuff like that."

"You mean like the haunted houses?"

"Oh, no. The kids don't say much about the haunted houses or the other things that go on. And even if they do, they don't go into the details. That's for their own fun, and they don't want to worry their parents. At least that's the way the kids who keep coming back feel about it, and as long as the kids like coming, the parents seem to like sending them. God knows what the kids who don't come back might be saying, but that doesn't matter anyway. No one's going to bellyache before they get home. They'd look like namby pamby assholes. And when the summer's over, it's over. Who cares what they say after the fact?"

The cool logic of this statement seemed incredible to Ted. He wanted to ask Mike more questions, but they were already at the rec hall. The moment they stepped inside, they were distracted.

The rec hall was ablaze with light. Entering it from the darkness was like entering a Western fantasy. The walls were decorated with spurs and Stetson hats. Some of the girls wore jeans and boots, but others wore those long, full skirts you sometimes see on TV when the commercial shows people square dancing. Some of the boys from other camps wore full Western outfits, everything from hats and shirts to silver-tipped boots. Ted wished they'd been told to look a little more Western—only a few of the guys had even worn cowboy boots. Then he realized that once the dancing began, it wouldn't matter much anyway.

With nothing yet going on, the Old West fantasy was marred by uneasiness. The girls were down at the far end of the room, where the fiddler was tuning up beside the caller. The boys from different camps stood around in their own groups, paying no attention to anyone, male or female, they didn't know. The Camp Loraine counselors were just finishing setting up the refreshment area, which had been made to look like an old-time saloon, complete with chairs, tables, and swinging doors. It took them and the other counselors to bring everyone together, and once squares had been formed and partners chosen, the evening began.

Ted found himself standing in front of an adorable, dark-haired girl, dressed in jeans and boots. She smiled, her full mouth and dark eyes lighting up her face. She was tall, but

74

not as tall as he.

She held out her hand. "I'm Sally Wren."

"Ted Jenner."

"Hi, Ted Jenner."

"Do you always introduce yourself by your full name?"

"Yes. Why?"

"A lot of people don't these days. More informal, I guess."

"My name is me. I like people to know the whole me from the start."

"I like that. I like you."

Sally blushed. "You only just met me."

"So what?"

"You don't know anything about me. In ten minutes, you could discover you hate everything I stand for."

"I hope you don't stand for anything. I just want you to be you."

"You know what I mean."

"Of course. But I like you anyway."

He was starting to like this girl a lot and starting to forget all those negative thoughts about Camp Cherokee. He hoped he wasn't carrying the banter too far, and that if he did, there would be some kind of warning to get him back on track. He needn't have worried. The fiddler burst into his first tune, and everyone began dancing.

Stamping his feet to the music, the caller, a tall man with a sharp face, really got them going. They honored their partners and their corners. They do-se-doed with their partners, swinging them high as they spun, arms linked. They do-se-doed with their corners and did a terrific allemande left, boys and girls clasping arms one to the next. But no matter where they happened to be in the dance, Sally had a special wink or a funny grin for Ted. And when they were together, they danced perfectly. Never a missed step or a moment's hesitation.

Suddenly, as the music soared, a couple broke free from a square and whirled around the room. "Whoopeee!" the boy shouted, and Ted knew at once it was Jack. The girl clung to him grimly, holding up the edge of her skirt.

The square Jack and his girl had broken out of had been forced to stop dancing, and now, realizing something odd was going on, the caller stopped calling, the fiddler stopped fiddling, and everything ground to a halt.

Music or not, Jack kept whirling. Then, when it began to seem ludicrous, he stopped.

Everyone stared. The girl pulled away and rushed to the other side of the room.

Jack grinned at the crowd and waved. "Hi, everybody," he said. "Having fun?" Then, like any movie bad guy, he plowed through the swinging doors of the saloon.

Ted was mortified.

Sally smiled up at him. "Friend of yours?"

"Well . . ."

"I like you better."

"Thanks."

The mood of shock and consternation blew off like smoke. The different squares regrouped. A counselor took Jack's place. The fiddler began again, and the rec hall was filled with the sound of clapping hands and stamping feet.

Jack didn't reappear for three dances. When he did, it was for a Virginia reel. He swaggered into line and did everything wrong. When it was time to move forward, he stood back. Instead of moving with his partner, he moved away. And when the two lines of boys and girls turned from each other and then regrouped, he stood still and had to be pushed aside.

A tall, broad-shouldered Camp Loraine counselor led him to the side of the room. Her words were whispered, but Ted saw Jack's face grow rigid as she spoke.

"Is this the way Cherokee boys usually behave?" said Sally.

"Sure," said Ted. "Only most of the time we break up the place."

Sally laughed. "You're breaking me up as it is."

The music stopped. It was time for refreshments. Squares dissolved. Couples dispersed. Conversation hummed.

Ted and Sally burst through the swinging doors, laughing. At the makeshift bar there was nothing but Coke and a murky grapefruit punch that looked as if it might be contaminated. They chose Coke and settled into a table in the corner. They held hands and talked about themselves.

Sally was from Ann Arbor, Michigan. Her father was a professor at the University, and she loved living on campus. Her mother was a schoolteacher, and she thought it was terrific that his mother taught, too, and that his father was an architect. She thought she might be interested in architecture herself.

Ted kept thinking about how much he was enjoying this, how embarrassing Jack had been, and how he'd seen Tim and Ricky hanging out behind the punch bowl but hadn't even wanted to say hello. The thought that Lee would have enjoyed something like tonight also briefly crossed his mind. He didn't know why exactly—Lee was probably too shy or too weird to start talking to any girls—but for some reason

77

it seemed suddenly sad and wrong that he got excluded from everything. He wasn't really that bad. Compared to Ricky Dunn, he was a prince.

He was about to say something about this to Sally when Jack leaned across the table and said "Hiii!"

Ted introduced him to Sally, but that wasn't good enough. Jack waved his cup of Coke in the air, spilling a little. "Sally," he said, "I've always loved that name. You won't mind if I sit down, will you?"

Before Ted could say anything, Jack squeezed in beside Sally and flung his arm around her.

Sally looked at Ted. Ted brushed the arm away.

"Hey, what's up?" Jack said.

"Nothing," Ted said. "Just cool it, please."

"Well," Jack said, "I don't think I'll disturb you lovebirds any longer. If you'll excuse me—"

He got up, and grabbed Ted by the shirt. "Just remember who I am," he said, and stalked off.

Sally touched Ted's cheek. "Are you all right?"

"Sure."

"That guy is weird."

"Weird is hardly the word. It's not easy to explain—"

"Don't even try."

The fiddler was starting up again. They'd done four more dances when Ted said, "How about a rest on the porch?"

Sally smiled her radiant smile. "For you, anything. Well, almost anything."

They both laughed. He followed her out. There was a wicker sofa at the far end. The music seemed muffled and far away. It was lovely being alone and quiet. They held hands. They kissed.

78

"I wish you didn't live in Michigan."

"It won't be so bad. I'll write to you. Maybe I'll even come to New York. I'll write to you in camp for a start."

He put his arms around her. They kissed again.

"Hey, lovebirds!" came the voice. "I thought I'd find you out here. What's the matter? Company not good enough inside?"

This was really pushing it. Jack capered down the porch, stopped short in front of them, bent over, smiled. "You're not trying to be antisocial, are you?"

The smile turned to a leer.

"Jack," Ted said, "would you please get out of here?"

"What?" said Jack.

Ted stood up. "I said—"

Jack grabbed him and pushed him against the wall. Ted grabbed back. Then Hambone appeared and pulled Jack away. "Hey," he said, "enough."

And they were gone.

Ted rearranged his clothes. "I'm sorry about this. I guess we'd better go inside."

"Kiss me one more time," said Sally.

Ten

"Won't someone from Camp Loraine talk to Mr. Bruce about Jack?"

Ted's question hung in the air. Just back from the dance, he and Hambone were sitting outside for a moment before going in to bed. Ted was on the top step of the cabin. Hambone stretched out a step below.

He shrugged. "Nah. Maybe. Who knows? Even if someone does, it won't matter. Bruce knows Jack is outrageous. He's always outrageous. Bruce'll just apologize and laugh and forget about it."

"Weren't you embarrassed?"

"Yeah, but it didn't matter. It was just a square dance. Some people thought he was funny."

"You didn't look so amused when you rescued me."

"You got the girl, didn't you? No harm done."

"We're going to write letters."

"Look, kid. Jack's the main man around here. He likes you. You're part of the group. You don't want to mess with that. So he isn't always sweet and charming. So big deal."

"What about the haunted-house stuff?"

"What about it? I don't go on those things. Remember, I'm out of camp a lot."

"Jack gets—I don't know. He was really crazy."

"No shit. What happened?"

"Put a kid in a potato sack. Threw him around. Beat him up."

Hambone laughed. "Any bones broken?"

"No."

"So forget it. House hauntings are supposed to be a little rough."

"But this kid was really hurt. And Jack didn't even care. He thought he'd done the right thing."

"And what should he have done?"

"I don't know. He didn't have to beat the kid so badly."

"And how did the kid feel about it?"

"Shit, he probably felt he was being braver because he got hurt."

"So? That's not really so bad. And the kid didn't check into the infirmary, did he? He didn't make a quick trip to the hospital?"

"No."

"So where's the harm?"

"I don't know. This logic is all Jack's logic. It's just not right."

Hambone stood to go inside. He punched Ted's shoulder. "Come on, kid. Believe me. None of this is really so terrible. It's all in your head."

Two nights later Ted knew Hambone was wrong.

They'd gathered together for another house haunting. Jack still hadn't said a word about the dance. Over dinner he'd asked Ted to come with him again.

The same group assembled at the mess hall: Jack and Ricky, Tim and Ted. Tim was barely speaking to Ted now. Ted couldn't have cared less.

Moving over to the ranchwagon in the dark, Jack was carrying two plastic bags.

"Whatcha got?" Ted asked.

Jack grinned. "A little something extra."

Ted was puzzled. Jack dumped the bags in the trunk and they were off.

It might have been Ted's imagination, but Jack's driving seemed improved. He didn't go so fast. He didn't hurtle around every curve. Who knows? Ted thought. Maybe he learned something the other night.

They were going to the Wilson house again. Tonight's group was Senior boys, tougher and older than the Intermediates. If Jack had decided to change his ways, it was a good moment to choose.

They parked in the same grove as before. It was just as dark and just as scary, but the grim, old house, the tall grass, and the terrible smell were all familiar now. Ted still had that feeling that someone unknown might loom out at him, but even that he had under better control.

Until Jack hung the dead cat over the stairway.

It was in one of the plastic bags. Jack went up the stairs first. As the others reached the landing, he shouted "Surprise!" and pulled out the cat.

Its eyes bulged. Its body was stiff in death. Everyone winced.

"Where did you get that?" Tim asked.

"Murphy, the cook, found him," Jack said. "He's been dead a couple of days."

"Oh, my God," Ted said.

"What's the matter? Squeamish?" said Ricky.

Jack ignored them both. He strung the cat up on a piece of twine. Then he directed everyone to their places.

Standing in the empty front room, Ted took note that Jack had not, as he'd suggested, asked him to take charge of the potato sack. Would there be a sack tonight? A Senior probably wouldn't fit into one.

The first kid came to the door, knocked, and got his B. The next one walked inside.

"Coming up," Ted whispered.

The kid started up the stairs. He was thin and rangy, not someone Ted knew. He recoiled at the sight of the cat, but it didn't stop him. As he reached the top step, Jack flicked on his flashlight. The beam struck the boy in the face. His hand flew over his eyes. At that moment Jack ripped open the other plastic bag and threw it.

It burst as it made contact, splattering the boy with chicken blood. "Aaaaaahhh!" he shouted, and ran.

There was a lull as Mr. Bruce looked after the terrified boy, wiped him off, and got his next victim ready to go. Too stunned to move, Ted tried not to throw up.

The next boy was so afraid, he never got near the house, but the one after that—a big, fat toughie—walked right in.

Past the rocker. Past the cat. Jack jumped the kid and punched him in the mouth. His lower lip split. He sat down hard, dropping his flashlight.

Jack danced around the figure on the blood-soaked floor. He made strange, whooping sounds. He and Ricky kicked the boy a couple of times, then pulled him to his feet. Ricky handed back the flashlight.

Hand on his arm, Jack led the boy into the front room. He motioned to Ted to do nothing.

"Shine your light through the window," he said, "for your B +."

The boy turned on his flashlight. A cheer went up from the road.

"Now get out of here. And remember you didn't see anyone."

He kicked the boy in the ass as he went, and when the next one came, after an interval of cowards rating Xs and XXs, he threw him down the stairs.

All the way home in the car, Ricky and Tim joked around with Jack. All the way home, Ted sat angrily in silence.

Eleven

He dreamed terrible dreams of bloody beatings. He had nothing to do with Jack. When Hambone asked him to come on down to the clearing in the woods, he said, "Thanks. I'm tired."

"Are you okay?"

"Yeah, fine."

"Jack still on your mind?"

"I guess."

"You're being foolish."

"I know."

Thursday morning Higg asked him to be an assistant group leader on Sunday's overnight horseback trip for Seniors. He'd just brought Nelly up to the riding field. He was hardly awake. But it would be his first overnight! He was ecstatic.

"I'd also like you to ride Jericho," Higg said.

Jericho was one of Higg's two hunters. No one but Higg ever rode him.

"Thanks," said Ted. "That's fantastic!"

Higg smiled. "You've been doing a good job. And the horse needs work."

There was a pause.

"You won't miss riding Nelly?"

"Of course I will. But I'll get over it."

Higg laughed dryly. "I suppose you will."

He sauntered off in that stiff, bowlegged way of his. He was such a good teacher, low-key and gritty, you couldn't help but like him. Even if he did go along with anything Jack wanted. But now there would be Jericho! And an overnight! What a perfect way to blot Jack out of his mind.

Or so he thought until he got to the stable. T. R. Bruce had the list of riders and their group assignments. "Oh, hi, Jenner," he said. "Group 5. Over by the road."

Ted went and saddled Jericho, a big, dark bay. Skittish even in his stall, he kept moving around as Ted tried to tighten the girth. Then he tossed his head and wouldn't take the bit.

Finally Ted led him out into the yard and mounted up. Jericho moved off before he had his feet in both stirrups. They ambled over to the road, the rich leather smell of Higg's tack delighting Ted's nostrils.

Jack Dunn slouched on Big Red's back, his right leg thrown over the pommel of his saddle. "Hi," he said, "haven't seen you the last few days."

"I've been around," Ted said. "I'm looking for Group 5."

"You came to the right place. I'm group leader."

"You?"

"You must be my assistant."

Oh, my God. "I guess so." Ted said.

Jack beckoned to him. "Listen, we'll have some fun."

Ted tensed. Jack went right on.

"I want to see how fast Jericho is. When we hit a good, flat stretch, we'll have a race."

"I don't think that's a good idea."

"I'm not giving you the choice."

Say something, anything. Ted pushed out the words. "Higg's not going to like it."

"We're the last group. No one will know. I give the signal. You let that sucker run."

As they started off, following the Old Glory Road through camp, Ted was rapidly losing enthusiasm. Taking up the rear, knowing the eight Senior boys between him and Jack were not the best riders, he got more and more nervous about a race.

As they passed the riding field, Hambone and a few Intermediate boys stepped out of the woods and applauded. "Have a good trip!" Hambone shouted.

Ted smiled and waved as Jericho pranced sideways. How he hoped against hope this trip might be a good one.

Down the hill they went and up another, and then down and across a flat stretch of fields. The first time Jack raised his hand to change the gait, Ted's heart stopped. But it was only a trot, and everyone did fine. Then they cantered for a while, a nice slow canter. Jericho tried to lunge ahead and finally plowed into the hind end of the horse in front of him when Jack suddenly called walk.

They walked through some woods, which helped to cool the horses and themselves on this hot, dry day. Ted felt a breeze blow past his cheek and luxuriated in it, it was so unexpected.

Moments later they were back in the sun, a sun so intense it was like an enemy. They cantered a little more and trotted, but the dust grew thicker and dryer and every time they picked up speed, they choked.

Two hours passed. The riders, though a little shaky, continued to do well. But everyone was tired and sweaty, and when Jack called a halt and dismounted, there were murmurs of relief all around.

Beside the road was a spigot, tapping a mountain spring into a huge rain barrel. How had it gotten there? No one knew, but the group was too thirsty to care.

Taking his turn last, holding in the urge to sweep everyone else aside, Ted drank deep from the dipper, then poured the water over his head. He had hardly ever felt so refreshed, the wet surrounding him with an aura of coolness that dissolved his fears as well as his fatigue. It was only then, with his sense of relaxation once more complete, that Jack announced the race.

Around the next bend were two miles of straight dirt. They were taking off.

The boys said nothing. Ted said nothing. Slowly everyone moved out.

They came around the bend. Jack reined in Big Red. He shot his fist into the air and cranked his arm four times. "Go!" he shouted, and was gone.

Even though he'd seen it coming, the sudden surge of energy took Ted by surprise. "No!" he shouted, but as Big Red took off, the other horses followed, and Jericho, suddenly, along with them.

Jericho ran easily behind the others. No urging, no use of the heels or voice, was necessary. The horse had wanted this all along.

His ears were pointed forward. He wanted to go faster and move ahead. How typical of Jack to start a race with himself in front. Well, if it was a race he wanted, Jericho would give him one.

Dirt and pebbles stung Ted's face. Dust was everywhere. He leaned forward in his saddle, nudged Jericho with his heels, and gave him his head. The horse took off like a shot.

Within fifty yards he'd passed all eight horses in the group. A couple of the boys had gotten into it and were urging their horses faster. A couple of others were smiling grimly, hanging in and waiting for this to be over. One, Jeff Kerr, looked scared to death. He was wobbling in the saddle and holding the pommel with both hands.

But Ted had to catch Jack! He turned his head away and instantly gained ten feet on Big Red. He was almost on his tail, Jericho's legs pounding beneath him, when he heard the scream.

He knew who it was without looking.

"Jack!" he shouted. "Wait!"

Jericho was going so fast, it was hard to slow him down. He pulled back on the reins, pulled harder, and gradually sat back in the saddle. As Jericho went slower, Ted could feel the horses behind him slowing, too. Finally they all stopped.

The boys were half out of their saddles. Bunched together. Horses lathered up and snorting. One saddle was empty.

A quarter mile back Jeff Kerr lay in the road.

Jack came up. "What happened?"

Ted pointed.

Jack smiled. "Let's go. Boys, wait here."

Jeff was sitting up when they reached him. Dust covered his clothes and hair. His shirt was torn on one side, his right arm badly scraped. But that seemed about it.

Jack helped him to his feet. "Are you okay?"

"Yes. I think so."

A little dazed. A moment or two to feel steady.

"Can you walk?"

"Yes."

And he did. By the time he and Jack had reached the others and Ted arrived leading Big Red and Jericho, Jeff was ready to go on.

"Good show," Jack said as he helped him onto his horse, patting him on the ass as his leg swung over. "You've got guts, Jeff."

And Jeff was pleased. He'd torn his shirt, scraped his arm, narrowly missed a concussion, and been frightened out of his wits, but there he was, smiling at Jack as if he were his best friend. Jack had been responsible for this mess and so, Ted realized with a shock, had he. But Jack, in his hero's role, had turned it into a triumph. How Ted hated him for that. If anything had remained of his good feelings for Jack, if anything had remained of the spell, it was all gone now.

They walked the horses dry, then trotted a couple of times and had one good, collected canter before they reached the campsite. Jeff Kerr came through it all splendidly, but when they rode into that open field and staked out a spot on the picket line for their horses, there was no way of concealing the torn shirt, the scraped arm, and the dried perspiration on the horses' flanks.

They were unsaddling and stacking the saddles when Higg appeared.

"Something happen?" he asked Jack.

"Jeff Kerr fell off. He'll be okay."

"That all?"

"Yup."

It was then that Higg gave Jack a look Ted had never

seen before. It was filled with admiration and mistrust, both accepting and accusing, and none of it made the slightest impression on Jack.

Higg looked at Ted the same way. Ted smiled nervously. He didn't know how to respond. But he realized, once and for all, that if he kept going along with Jack, he'd be stuck with looks like that and a bad conscience.

He went to bed early. The ranchwagon had come with the boys' bedrolls and food. They'd fed the horses on the picket line and grilled hamburgers and corn over the campfire. Then they'd drawn straws for picket-line duty, one hour each all through the night, and Ted had drawn two to three. After the events of the day, he figured that if he were going to get any sleep at all, he'd better get to it.

For a while he lay looking at the stars. The horses were chewing hay and stomping their feet. Flames danced as the campfire died down. Voices gently murmured. He was asleep before he knew it.

He woke, startled. Someone had punched him in the shoulder. A dark shape above his sleeping bag. Tall, loose, hands on hips. It could only be one person.

"Wake up," Jack said. "I need you."

"What time is it?"

"Around one. Come on. Come with me."

He wanted to say no. He went.

The night was perfectly still and cold. The campfire had burned down to crackling embers. The guys on picket-line duty huddled around it, drinking coffee from their mess-kit cups.

"Quiet," Jack said, as they approached the horses.

Stumbling along, still groggy with sleep, Ted wasn't about

to say anything anyway. He felt chilled and out of sorts. In an hour he'd be up again.

Tied on either side of the long rope strung between posts, the horses went on grazing. Jack ducked under the rope and released the horse nearest him. Then he backed it up and shooed it into the woods.

"What's the point?" Ted asked.

"I want to fix the kid riding Champion."

"The guys on the picket line will notice. They'll just find Champion and tie him up again."

"They'll blame the kid."

"So what?"

"Come on. There's more."

"You don't need me for this."

"Yes, I do."

"What's the kid done?"

"Don't worry about it."

At the far end of the picket line, feedbags were stacked. Jack grabbed one and tossed another to Ted.

"Fill this with rocks," Jack said. "The bigger, the better."

"No!" said Ted. "I don't want to."

Jack grabbed Ted by the throat. His face was shiny and alive with hate. "You do what I tell you. You hear me?"

Fear shot through Ted. Alone with this madman in the cold dark, he began to sweat. He followed Jack into the woods. Finding rocks without a flashlight wasn't easy. They hunted under trees and down a slope. It took about twenty minutes to fill the feedbags.

"Okay," Jack said when they were done, "Group 2's across the field. This kid's got a surprise coming."

"I don't want to do this," Ted said.

"Just do it, Ted."

"I don't even know this kid. We might hurt him."

Jack grinned. It was the same grin Ted had seen that first evening near the mess hall, the same grin he had seen so many times since. Only now Jack was grinning at the thought of violence and pain and revenge. He was going to enjoy hurting this boy, in the same way he'd enjoyed beating up those kids at the haunted house and pushing Lee down in the watering trough. He was, Ted realized, capable of murder, and what he wanted was a flunky along to help, no questions asked. Well, the flunky had had enough. The flunky was going to stop him!

Ten sleeping bodies. Jack found the one he wanted. Ted was right beside him.

The boy stirred in his sleep.

Jack hoisted the feedbag over his head. "Now!" he whispered.

Ted knocked the bag out of Jack's hands. The boy shot up. "What's going on?"

Ted dropped his bag of rocks and ran. Blood pounded in his head. Behind him Jack was swearing.

When they reached the woods, Jack caught him and threw him down. "What do you think you were doing?" he snarled.

The ground was wet and hard. "I couldn't let you do that," Ted gasped.

"It wasn't up to you."

"You would have hurt him. You could have killed him! You wanted me to hurt him, too."

"It was a prank. *My* choice!"

"It wasn't just a prank. It was awful. And you got me to

come. You've got no right to choose for me!"

"Is that so?"

"Yeah!"

Jack sat on Ted's chest. He pinned his arms with his hands. Ted felt he would be crushed into the ground, crushed and turned into earth and dead leaves. Jack's words drove into him like spears.

"Let me tell you something, Jenner. I make the rules, and you've been a pain in the ass. I liked you. I gave you a break. But I've had it. Try something like this again, and I'll bust your head!"

Twelve

On picket line duty that night, walking endlessly around the horses, Ted thought about Jack and how wrong he'd been about him. How easy it was to accept his overtures and be led along by his magnetism when all he really offered was the chance to do his dirty work.

Well, no more. But what about Jack's group? He liked some of the people, liked going to the secret clearing, liked being "in." If he could just avoid Jack, it might be okay.

Impossible. He had stopped Jack once. He had to try and stop him for good. But what could he do? Higg and all the counselors were under Jack's thumb, and even if they weren't, they all knew T. R. Bruce thought Jack was God. They'd never say anything against him. What about Doug Parelli? Nah, Doug would just give him a hug and turn the whole thing into a joke. The real trouble was that only the victims and the accomplices knew the truth, and they wouldn't do anything either.

Funny, how Lee had been right about Jack all along.

In the morning, emerging once more from warm sleeping bags into cold mountain air, it was as if nothing unusual had happened. Jack was his cordial, commanding self, and he and Ted went around together, making sure their group had fed and groomed their horses and cooked up a lot of bacon and eggs for themselves. Beyond that it was into the saddle and back to camp before lunch.

The ride was uneventful. In fact, as they pulled into the stable, Ted heard Jeff Kerr, right arm bandaged, say, "Gee, we didn't even have another race."

The perfect example of Jack's theory in action.

But Ted couldn't let the matter rest. Now that he was back in camp, his sense of urgency increased.

What if he did what no counselor would do? What if he went and talked to Mr. Bruce? Sure, Bruce was in cahoots with Jack and thought he was great, but Jack himself had said Bruce didn't know all the details of what went on. He would take convincing, but if Ted just went in and calmly, reasonably, presented those details, maybe. . .

He thought about this through lunch and rest hour. When everyone went off to free play, he went to the administration building.

T. R.'s secretary was not at her desk. On the off chance Mr. Bruce was in, Ted knocked on his office door.

"Come in," said the voice.

Mr. Bruce sat behind an elegant mahogany desk. The desk chair and the chair opposite were matching brown leather. The walls were lined with books. On the floor was a blue and gold Oriental rug.

The office was so unusual for a camp director, Ted was taken aback, and when Mr. Bruce smiled, motioned him to the empty chair, and said, "Why, Jenner, how nice to see you," he didn't know how to begin.

The leather of the chair was soft and comfortable. The room was cozy.

Mr. Bruce said, "You wanted to talk?"

"Yes," Ted said.

"You're having a good summer at Cherokee, I hope."

"Yes."

"I've noticed you doing real well with that Nelly. She's always been a handful, but I don't think she will be for long."

"Thank you, sir."

"Higg, Jack Dunn—they have nothing but good things to say about you."

The "other people" from Director's Inspection. Wait till T. R. got the next installment from Jack. Hang on a minute. That's why he was here!

"Mr. Bruce—"

"Yes, Ted." He laughed. "It's not the food, I hope. We're getting a new supplier. Murphy tells me next week will make all the difference, and I can usually trust his word."

He trusted Jack's word, too. It made so little sense. Jack was just a camper, and he got away with everything. He had everyone's trust and did nothing but abuse it. But it was so comfortable in this chair, so pleasant in this room, so enjoyable talking to Mr. Bruce, who praised him. Jack probably wouldn't say anything anyway. He wouldn't want anyone to know they'd quarreled. But Jack was crazy. He could kill someone!

"So," Mr. Bruce said.

Ted opened his mouth to speak. Mr. Bruce smiled again.

"If you've got questions about Old Glory Road Night, I save all those for the occasion. Can't believe it's almost here. Just a few more days."

"No," said Ted, "it wasn't about that. It was about Jack."

Mr. Bruce leaned back in his chair. He joined his fingers

at the tips and smiled his inscrutable, gray smile. "My old friend Jack," he said. "I know what he does might strike some people as a bit unusual, a bit, shall we say, unorthodox, but Jack, you know, is responsible for a lot of what makes Camp Cherokee run so smothly and so well. He may be just a camper, but he's a great deal more than that to me. He's a part of our Cherokee tradition, a tradition I'm very proud of. But what was it you wanted to say about him?"

It was useless. A stone wall had gone up. Ted sat there listening to this glowing tribute to Jack Dunn and wanted to cry. When it was over, he couldn't even look at Mr. Bruce. He said nothing.

Mr. Bruce stood up. "Well," he said, "I guess you've changed your mind. But I'm glad you stopped by, and I'm glad you're enjoying your summer."

He held out his hand.

Ted stood up and took it.

Cold feet! How could he have gone into Mr. Bruce's office, sat right in front of him, and been overwhelmed by words? He should have expected a speech like that. He'd behaved like an idiot.

He'd be too embarrassed to go in a second time. He stormed up and down the floor of the cabin. What to do now. Free play was almost over. This afternoon there was a basketball game, Horsemen against Seniors. He had no time to think.

The door burst open.

"Hey, hey," said Hambone, "why weren't you down at archery just now. Three bull's-eyes in a row. You didn't know I was that good."

"No, I didn't," said Ted. "Next thing you'll be telling me you're part Indian."

"I am," said Hambone. "I'm surprised I didn't tell you that before."

He went whooping around in a circle just as the door burst open again. There were Lee and Tim, followed by Doug Parelli, with the message: "Shorts and sneakers, please. Ten minutes till game time."

Activity followed activity over the next few days, and Ted allowed himself to be distracted by each of them. And why not? he continued to ask himself. This was camp. It was supposed to be fun. The only person creating an issue was himself.

But as those days passed, one subject became *the* subject on everyone's lips. Ted had heard about it before. He'd heard about it again in T. R. Bruce's office. Old Glory Road Night.

One afternoon, when the residents of Cabin 3 were lying around during rest hour, he asked Doug Parelli for details.

"A hundred years ago," Doug said, "some guy got murdered on the Old Glory Road. T. R. decided to make a big deal of it."

"And?"

"Everyone buys a ticket, starts out at the stable, walks down to Old Glory Barn, gets a note, and comes back to the mess hall."

"That's it?"

"That's it."

"Not quite," said Tim.

"What do you mean?" Ted asked.

"There are obstacles," said Tim.

"What kind of obstacles?"

"You'll find out."

"It's worse than that," said Lee. "Anyone can steal your note if you get one."

"You have to hide it in a good place," said Hambone. He laughed.

"You can't leave the road," said Lee.

"They cream you if you do," said Tim.

"The winners split the pot," said Doug.

"There aren't many winners," said Tim.

All this sounded like a weird chorus, preparing Ted for yet another tragedy. But no matter how many questions he asked, everything about Old Glory Road Night remained a little vague. Every camper went—it was another of T. R. Bruce's tests for cowardice—so all the old campers knew what went on. But there seemed to be some delight in keeping the actual happenings from anyone "going down the road" for the first time.

This was either part of the fun, part of the agony, or— maybe—there were more people pretending they knew what went on than did. Tim had said there weren't many winners. Ted began to suspect that a lot of people didn't make the whole trip.

But why would that be? And what was Jack's role? Old Glory Road Night seemed tailor-made for Jack Dunn.

By the time Thursday night rolled around, Ted felt both terrified and helpless. As he walked down to the stable in his navy blue parka—you had to wear a dark color and carry no flashlight—he struck up a conversation with Bob Colter. Bob was another first-year Horseman, barrel-chested, with a shock of brown hair he was always pushing out of his eyes.

"Well, what do you think?" Ted asked.

"How do I know?" said Bob. "I'd like to be home in bed."

"Think you'll win?"

"Doubt it."

"Why not?"

"Just a feeling."

"How do you feel right now?"

"Scared shitless. How else?"

They both laughed and slapped each other on the back. At least there are two of us, Ted thought, but as they entered the bright light of the main barn and he saw the tense, dark faces looking up at him, he knew there were many more.

Hambone and Tim were sitting cross-legged in a corner. Tripping over several legs, struggling across the floor packed with bodies, Ted joined them.

"Hi," he said, sitting where there was barely room to sit.

"Welcome to the loony bin," said Hambone.

"Why Hambone," said Ted, "don't tell me you're not happy about this latest example of Cherokee tradition."

"Happy?" said Hambone. "Can't you tell I'm overjoyed?"

"Oh, come on, Hambone," said Tim. "The whole thing's fun. All this being scared is just a crock."

"That may be true for you, Superman, but *I've* never made it back with a note."

"Last year was a snap," said Tim. "Just relax and enjoy yourselves."

"I was more relaxed before I got here," said Hambone.

By now all the campers had arrived. Ted saw Lee sitting alone near the far wall. He thought of calling him over—

he still hadn't told him he was right about Jack—but too late. Up in front, Mr. Bruce was getting ready to speak.

"Hey," Tim whispered as the room turned quiet, "good luck, you guys. Maybe we'll all split the pot."

He held out his hand, first to Hambone, then to Ted.

Hambone mumbled something unintelligible. "Thanks, Tim," Ted said. "Good luck to you, too."

He was amazed. And the gesture seemed even bolder because Tim had won before and they would be competing directly against one another. Could things be changing? Could Tim have decided he wanted to be friends?

"Welcome, welcome, welcome," Mr. Bruce said, holding his arms out over the group as if he were giving some strange benediction. "As those of you who have done this before are aware, you will all be having a most unusual experience tonight. Before we begin, as I do every year at this time, I would like to relate some history."

Bathed in light, framed against the dark entrance to the barn, Mr. Bruce had an almost spectral quality. His eyes gleamed, the corners of his mouth flicked upward, and, as he spoke to the boys crowded on the floor, the atmosphere in the room turned to ice.

It seemed that on this July date, in the summer of 1893, one Oliver Turpin started down the Old Glory Road just before dark. Carrying his biweekly payroll, he was bound for the stone quarry he owned near where the Old Glory Barn now stands. He never made it. In the gully of the Old Glory Road, his carriage was stopped, and he was set upon, robbed, and murdered. When he failed to appear on schedule, his workers went looking for him. They discovered his body, stabbed in the heart, in the gully of the Old Glory

Road. Two weeks later, Burton Blackwell, an unemployed laborer, was arrested for the crime. The evidence was mostly circumstantial, but the jury didn't care. They convicted Burton Blackwell, and he was hanged before the year was out.

"And now," Mr. Bruce said, "every year on the night of the twenty-sixth of July, the ghost of poor, murdered Oliver Turpin haunts the gully of the Old Glory Road. And the ghost of Burton Blackwell, justly or unjustly accused we will never know, swings eerily from a branch of a nearby tree. To do this sad event honor and to catch a glimpse of those unhappy ghosts, we conduct our walk each year."

Ted couldn't quite understand why this murder and those ghosts should be honored or why honoring them made it necessary to walk down the Old Glory Road in the middle of the night. But contrary to what Mr. Bruce had suggested in his office, no questions were being allowed anyway. The first name had already been called.

He was a skinny, Intermediate kid in a leather jacket. He had to step over a lot of legs to reach Mr. Bruce, and, by the time he did, his knees were shaking so hard he could barely stand. As Mr. Bruce took his ticket and sent him out into the night, he looked as if he were being sent to certain death.

Gradually, at one-minute intervals, more boys disappeared outside. But just as the crowd had been oppressive, the thinning of the crowd was that much worse. There had been safety in numbers, protection in a well-filled space. Now the emptiness revealed you, made you feel naked and exposed.

Ted, Hambone, and Tim clustered together.

"Ted Jenner!"

Ted's stomach clenched. He nodded his good-byes and walked forward.

Mr. Bruce remained impassive. No smile, no reference to the other day as he took Ted's ticket and ushered him into the night.

It took a moment for Ted's eyes to adjust. Then he crossed the hardtop and started up the Old Glory Road past camp.

Behind a row of trees, the lights of camp—the mess hall, the infirmary—had a special glow. They beckoned, but he said no.

Thirteen

Shadows. No stars. Pale wisps of cloud passing overhead. Their journey, whatever it was, seemed more comprehensible than his.

It was getting colder. He zipped his parka. He could see the back of the kid ahead of him. Then the kid vanished into the woods at the top of the hill past the riding field.

He reached the edge of the riding field himself—and heard a low, dirty laugh off to the right. He turned and got a blast of water in the face!

The water soaked him. The shock nearly sat him down. Someone had hooked up a hose to the watering trough.

He passed the top of the hill. The woods closed over him, and he started down. Fifty yards ahead, he was caught in a web.

The long, silken filaments were strung across the road. In a moment they had wrapped themselves around him, dozens of tiny electric shocks reverberating in his body.

He fought the wires, fought the shocks as they invaded him, hurting him more because he was wet. He plunged through them, as if he were plunging through a bead curtain, tripped and fell into a pile of manure spread across the road.

He lay there a minute, trying to regain composure. The

smell and feel of the manure were too familiar to bother him much. The shocks that had jarred his nerves died away. Whoever was behind him had either not shown up yet or had slipped away to his cabin, undisturbed. He rose, bits of manure clinging to his wet pants and jacket, the water sloshing in his shoes.

He went on down the hill.

It was a clammy feeling, walking in the cold in these wet clothes. But worse than that was the dark. The woods were so dense it was almost impossible to see. Every so often there was a grunt from the side of the road or the sound of a broken twig. When he turned toward the sounds, he saw nothing.

He had no idea where the men came from when they came. There were two of them, with strong arms that reached out and threw him to the ground. He looked up and noticed they were counselors, counselors he didn't know.

They were trying to strip him!

He resisted, wrenching his body this way and that, arching his pelvis and kicking with his feet. His arms were pinned to his sides, but he got them free and lashed out, delivering blows where he could.

They'd gotten his belt undone, and the laces on one of his shoes. They'd pulled his shirt out of his pants, but they couldn't get his parka off.

"Forget the clothes," Ted heard. "Just take him."

They grabbed his arms and legs. He went on struggling, but hoisted in the air, he had no leverage. He was carried the rest of the way down the hill, to what had to be the gully, then turned to the right and dumped on the grass.

Before him was the oddest structure he had ever seen. Only about three feet high but extending far back into the woods, it was made entirely of branches tied together with rope. A stockade, Ted realized, and inside, packed tight, were naked boys.

"Toss him in," said a voice, muffled but familiar.

A small door was lifted. The counselors grabbed Ted and shoved him through. He rammed into a cluster of arms and legs.

The stockade had a manure floor. All these squirming boys were naked in horse shit!

"Oh, no!" he heard behind him.

Boys began writhing away from the walls of the stockade on both sides. They piled on top of each other, gouging eyes, bumping chins.

With arms and legs and heads coming at him from all directions, Ted couldn't figure out what was going on. Then he saw. Every few feet on either side, someone was sticking a cattle prod through the slats.

When this had happened a second time and kids were crying and yelling and calling to go home, Ted couldn't take any more. As two kids were pushed in through the door, he crawled to the front of the stockade. He peered out through the slats.

Under a tree, two figures stood smoking cigarettes, cattle prods under their arms. No wonder that voice had seemed familiar. There was no mistaking Jack and Ricky Dunn.

Ted was mad now, mad and determined. Damn Jack and his viciousness! He'd get out of this stockade, get a note, and win!

Next time a beaten, naked boy was shoved in through

107

the door, he was ready. He pushed out after him, pushed up and out and took off.

The counselors watching the stockade were taken by surprise. Before they realized what had happened, Ted was at the road.

He stopped short. Standing in the gully was a wraithlike creature in a long black cowl. "Murder, murder," he said, over and over.

Ted grimaced. Someone was dressed up as the ghost of Oliver Turpin!

He was through the gully in a moment. A glance at the trees showed no swinging corpse of Burton Blackwell. T. R. Bruce and Company had fallen down on the job.

He started up the second hill. But someone else was coming down it! Would the kid think he was after his note? It didn't matter. All he wanted was his own.

The boy veered wide to the left. How eerie to have someone suddenly afraid of you. Jack would have loved it.

The rest of the hill was strangely quiet. It was as if, having come through the earlier horrors, he was now entitled to his rite of passage.

He walked quickly, and there, in a field, was Old Glory Barn.

Silhouetted against the night sky, the long-abandoned structure, still perfectly intact, looked gray and overbearing. Ted swept through the high grass. Monty Benson was standing at the front door, hands in the pockets of his dark green sweatsuit.

Ted laughed. "I didn't think you ever left the waterfront."

"I don't," said Monty. He made weird gestures with his arms. "This is my ghost you're seeing."

They laughed and shook hands. Both blond, both tall and thin, they could have been brothers.

"But what are you doing down here?" Ted asked.

"No one gets out of working on *the road*, my friend."

"Do you know what's going on in the gully?"

"You mean the stockade and stuff? It was all Jack's idea. Pretty gruesome, if you ask me."

"Why didn't someone say no to Jack?"

"What a question. T. R. gave his approval. You want brownie points in this place, you do what T. R. says."

"Did he know about the cattle prods?"

"Is that what they've got down there?"

"That's what they've got."

"Holy shit! Look, kid, you can't stand around talking. Take your note. Get out of here."

"Lot of guys get to the barn?"

"Not a lot. But you're going to make it. I'd take bets."

"Thanks. Thanks a lot."

"Congratulations in advance," said Monty.

So much for social conscience. No one was going to tell T. R. that Jack had gone too far. No one even wanted to think about it!

Back on the road. Covered by woods. Should he hide the note? Pointless. If someone was going to take it, someone was going to take it. He put it in his pocket.

There was someone coming up the road from the gully. Now he was the one to feel hunted. Gripped by fear, the other boy—it looked like Jim Burns—hardly noticed him.

How many kids would fight him for his note? Were they lining up along the road?

He was at the gully. The dark figure in the cowl stood,

moaning. Ted got past him and was grabbed from behind.

"Give me your note, sonny, and be quick about it."

Ted struggled. The grip on his arm was tight. "No," he said.

"You'd better," from beneath the cowl.

Ted pulled his arm away and ran. A look back. A face. It was Bruce Halpern, the riflery counselor.

He got partway up the hill back to camp and realized he wasn't supposed to be running. It was against the rules. He stood for a moment, catching his breath.

Then he heard the scream.

It came from back down the hill near the gully. As he listened, it came again.

He was running now, running in the direction of the scream. The rules were no longer important. This sounded like agony.

He reached the gully, sidestepped the ghost of Oliver Turpin, and headed for the stockade. Out back, stark naked against a tree, stood Lee Fischer. A rotten tree branch was in his hands. In front of him, wielding the cattle prod, was Jack Dunn.

Every time Jack lunged, Lee took a swipe at him. Lee kept missing, but Jack did not. Each time the cattle prod struck home, Lee screamed.

"Go ahead, scream," Jack snarled. "I hate you. I want everyone to hate you. You and your ugly face, your stupid pigheadedness. I want you to hurt!"

Another thrust with the cattle prod. Another scream from Lee. Lee's face was turning red and rubbery now, his mouth a grim slit.

Ted never paused. He raced across the grass.

"You son of a bitch!" he shouted. "Let him go!"

As Jack turned, surprised, Ted tackled him.

"Run!" he shouted. "Get out of here!"

Lee took off into the woods. Ted jumped up and ran back to the road.

He still had a note. He still had to stay on the road and get back to the mess hall.

He hadn't gone ten feet when two counselors were on him. They wrestled him to the ground. First they searched his mouth. Then they started going through his pockets.

"Here it is," said one. "He didn't even hide it."

"Poor sucker," said the other. "Let him up now."

"Hey," said the first, "isn't this the Jenner kid?"

"Shit, I think so."

"Isn't he—?"

"Yeah. Put it back."

They shoved the note back in Ted's pocket. They pushed him down and got out of there fast.

Ted lay where they'd left him. There had been the stockade and Jack and Lee. And now there was this.

No one who walked the road won because he deserved to win. The kids who won were the kids who were allowed to win! Somehow this act of treachery was as bad or worse than the others. No wonder Monty was so confident Ted would make it.

He wouldn't go to the mess hall. He'd do what half the kids in camp must have done by now. Go back to the bunk.

He left the road for the woods. The undergrowth was thick and hard to negotiate in the dark, and it took a while to grope his way forward. A couple of kids dashed behind trees as he passed, but he paid no attention.

He reached the cabin. No lights were on, but he could hear someone moving around. He was about to climb the steps when he realized he couldn't let go yet. He had to know the winners.

He shivered. His clothes were almost dry, but the temperature had dropped some more in the last hour. He could go in and change first, but the person in the cabin was probably Lee, and he didn't want to see Lee yet. Later, yes, but not now.

He walked up to the mess hall and through the swinging doors. He'd been in the dark and cold for so long, the light and heat seemed almost alien.

Benches and tables had been pushed back to the walls. A crowd of people—campers and counselors alike—surrounded T. R. Bruce in the middle of the room.

Ted's timing had been perfect. Mr. Bruce tapped on the microphone for silence. Then he announced the first three winners.

Ted knew he shouldn't have been shocked, but he was. Tim Fairchild, Ricky Dunn, Mike Schroeder. No wonder Tim had been friendly at the barn! He already knew he'd win again. And Ricky Dunn hadn't even walked down the road. He'd been busy with his cattle prod.

Someone came up beside him. He knew who it was without looking. He wished he'd chosen to stand in the crowd instead of across the room beside a pillar.

Jack said, "Why don't you get up there?"

"What do you mean?"

"Don't bullshit me, Ted. We know you've got a note."

"What makes you so sure?"

Jack stepped in front of Ted.

"You'd better get up there! If you know what's good for you!"

"I don't take orders from you, Jack!"

Almost without realizing it, Ted saw himself form his right hand into a fist. And then, almost in slow motion, he saw himself throw the punch at Jack.

Jack caught Ted's fist in his left hand. He slammed him up against the pillar.

"Listen to me, wise guy. I gave you one more chance, and you blew it. You're in trouble now, big trouble."

Ted choked back the tears. His side hurt. He wondered why not a single person in the mess hall had noticed what was going on. But T. R. Bruce was still talking, probably announcing another patsy.

Jack pushed him away. "See you around."

Ted grabbed his shoulder. "I'll get you, Jack!"

Jack grinned.

Fourteen

Ted raced out of the mess hall. He raced past the tennis courts and across the lawn to the cabins. He lost his footing and sprawled in the wet grass, but it didn't matter. He picked himself up and kept on running until he reached Cabin 3, Horseman Division. He burst through the door shouting "Lee, Lee, are you there?"

Lee looked up from his bunk. "Yeah, I'm here."

Ted bounded across the room. "I'm sorry, Lee. It was Jack, Jack all the time. I should have listened to you. I was so dumb."

Lee sat up in bed.

"And I'd like to be friends," Ted was saying. "Do you still want to?"

"Yes," said Lee. "I'd like that."

"Good, I'm glad."

They shook hands.

"What about Jack?" Lee asked.

"I don't think," Ted said, "that Jack's very interested in my friendship any longer."

He described what had happened in the mess hall. Then he described the haunted-house trips and the overnight.

"And, of course, there was your rescue."

"Thank you for that," said Lee. "If you hadn't shown

up, I'd have been in really bad shape."

"What seems most incredible is that no one else tried to stop him. But that's Jack for you. No one would."

"I guess not. But all this other stuff is really too much. He just goes around beating people up! He's really evil!"

"It's a wonder he hasn't killed anyone yet. Then he does a couple of good deeds and pours on the charm to keep everyone off-balance."

"And the whole road thing is a setup?"

"You got it."

"But what can we do?"

"About the road, not much. About everything else, I don't know. The real problem is T. R. Bruce knows everything except the awful details. And he thinks Jack is wonderful."

"I was aware of that. And, of course, not one of our knucklehead counselors would be any help. They wouldn't even tell what they knew, much less what they didn't know before you told them."

"It seems so weird, though. You'd think there would be one, just one—the kid isn't a magician with a wand, for God's sake! Though I can certainly imagine not wanting to take on T. R. Bruce. I didn't do so well myself on that score."

Ted described his experience in Mr. Bruce's office.

"Wow!" said Lee. "Into the lion's den!"

"Yeah," said Ted, "and right back out again. I don't know. You'd think someone like Higg wouldn't be so much in Jack's back pocket. I know he is, but—"

Lee looked away. "I thought so, too. A couple of years ago, I tried to talk to him about Jack and me. He was really

115

pissy about it. All he did was defend Jack. That's how I got on the wrong side of him in the first place."

"You mean that's where it all started between you and Higg?"

"Yup. Until then he hardly knew I existed."

"Score one more for Jack."

"I'll say. But what are we going to do about him? We're really stuck."

"We'll have to think. He's really going to be after me now."

"At least we have each other."

Ted paused, listening in his mind to what Lee had just said. He really hadn't liked this kid. He had mouthed words of friendship and appreciated it when Lee was nice to him, but all the while he had been put off by the infuriating things Lee had done. Now he had come to understand that a lot of those things had been in response to the image Jack had created. And he had changed his mind about Lee. He wanted to be friends with him. Thank God there was someone. There wasn't going to be anyone else.

"Yes," he said. "We have each other."

With Old Glory Road Night past, the tension that had developed to such a pitch beforehand disappeared. And everyone felt the letdown.

Ted couldn't have been more pleased. With no one carrying on about some major event, it became possible to concentrate on other things. Higg's lessons in the ring continued to be terrific. Nelly was getting calmer and calmer and seemed likely to become a fair polo pony. And arts and crafts, his replacement for riflery for the second half of the summer, had turned out to be sort of fun.

Ted still spent time with Hambone, when he was around, and with the other kids who'd made him so popular, but since Hambone and Tim weren't interested in Lee, and Ted was hardly welcome when they hung out with Jack, he found himself alone with Lee more and more.

It had begun that first morning after Old Glory Road Night. They'd sat next to one another at breakfast and exchanged disgusted looks as Tim went on about having won for the second straight year.

"Well, how about you, Ted?" he asked, when no one had any questions. "How far did you get last night?"

Ted smiled gamely. "I would have won, Tim," he said, "except I swallowed my note."

"You what?" said Tim.

"I squashed my note up real small. Then I put it in my mouth. And I swallowed it by mistake."

Tim looked appalled.

"Of course, if anyone wants to follow me around and see if anything turns up—"

Ted and Lee burst out laughing. When they left the mess hall, they were still talking about Tim's outraged face.

They went to the barn together. They went to group activities together. It turned out that Lee knew a lot about horse diseases, much more than Ted ever had. So Ted listened as Lee went on at length about mange and colic and the heaves and God knows what else. Once, on the way to the waterfront, Lee said, "Hey, Ted, you know any good restaurants in New York?"

"Sure," said Ted. "A few."

"Do you know the Omnibus? It's this great place in Greenwich Village."

"No."

"We'll have to go. When I'm in the city."

It began to seem like a friendship that would last that long. They began talking about disagreements with their parents and what their lives were like back home.

They'd been talking about Ted's chances for student government president when he said, "You know, this camp is so weird in so many ways, but the weirdest thing of all is that no one talks about home. I know Hambone comes from New Jersey. I know Jack comes from Pittsburgh and Tim comes from Chicago. But that's about all I know about any of these guys, apart from what they're like at camp."

"It's true," said Lee. "You get here. You talk a little about what happened over the winter. And that's it. The door closes. Nothing's important that doesn't go on at camp."

"You know, I got that kind of impression the first moment I arrived. Everything was beautiful, but it was so self-contained, so isolated. I felt I might never have any contact with the world again."

"That's the whole idea. And everyone inside can try to be anything he wants to be. Damn what he might have been back home. Damn that I was a brain with only two real friends. None of it's going to matter. No one will even know. You can do fine as long as you don't run up against Jack Dunn."

"What about Jack? Do you think he's this well-behaved honor student back in Pittsburgh?"

"Somehow I doubt it. I'd hate to be in his class at school. Ten months' worth of hell. Can you imagine?"

"Sure. Let's see. In October Jack forces everyone to put razor blades in candy bars and go trick-or-treating with him.

In November Jack stuffs the teacher's turkey with horseshit. In December, as Santa Claus . . ."

Lee started to laugh. So did Ted. It was the kind of shared laughter only real friends could enjoy.

They also talked about girls.

"I like them," Lee said at one point. "They just don't seem to like me."

Ted had realized that Lee was fine, as long as he wasn't made defensive. "You need to take it easy," he said. "Same as with everything else."

"That's easy for you to say. You're the big ladies' man."

"Oh, come on," said Ted. "It's not like that. Besides, Lynn wanted to break up with me as much as I wanted to break up with her."

"Sure, sure. Ever hear from that girl at the dance?"

"Oh, my God! I never wrote Sally. I promised to write first."

"Better get to it. You'll lose your reputation."

"Don't be smart."

While all this was going on, Ted kept wondering about Jack. He was around, the way he was always around, but apart from the occasional ugly look, he did nothing. It began to seem as if he might just leave them alone.

Then it was Ted's birthday.

He hadn't really thought about it. He'd had so much on his mind and been involved in so many things, it kind of sneaked up on him unexpectedly. Besides, in earlier summers he'd always celebrated in upstate New York. One year his friends gave him a party. Another year he went out to dinner with his parents. It seemed weird to be having a birthday at camp.

His parents sent a large box and a small one. He opened them both during rest hour. The large one was a new pair of shiny black riding boots with hunting tops. Everyone but Tim oohed and aahed.

"All set for the horse show," said Doug Parelli.

"I guess," said Ted, overwhelmed.

The smaller box was chocolates for the bunk. Ted passed it around. In a minute there was nothing left.

Ted held up the empty box. "You guys sure are pigs."

"Oink! Oink!" echoed around the room.

By midafternoon, what had been a bright, sunny day suddenly turned dark and threatening. By dinner, it was pouring. Still, as he put on his poncho and his moccasins and set out for the mess hall, Ted was eagerly anticipating his cake. Every birthday camper, he knew, got a special birthday cake to share with his bunk. As long as he led the whole camp in a song first.

"Ted Jenner! Ted Jenner, please!"

T. R. Bruce was at the microphone. As Ted got up from his bench, with several jokers whistling and applauding, the whole camp burst into "Happy Birthday."

Ted was embarrassed. He was also pleased. He got to the microphone and looked out at the mass of faces that were now, briefly, his.

"Let's all sing 'The Moonshiner Song.'"

As one, the mess hall burst into the opening verse:

> *I've been a Moonshiner*
> *For many a year*

I've spent all my money
On whiskey and beer. . . .

The song went on and on. It rang in Ted's ears as he pretended to conduct. Such a short while ago he had tried to identify Jack Dunn with the wonderful, reckless energy that came pouring out of this song. Now all he could see was the foul, old moonshiner behind the words.

He wondered where Jack was at this moment. He couldn't find him at his table. The song was drawing to a close. Mr. Bruce was hovering behind him.

He took the microphone. "Thank you, Ted. It was good to have some cheer on a stormy evening."

He paused a moment, and, as if on cue, the wind howled around the mess hall and the rain beat down on the roof.

"Before we give Ted his cake," Mr. Bruce went on, "I have a brief announcement to make. A letter has come into my hands. We're not entirely sure whose it is, but the contents are very interesting. I'm going to read some of it now. Would the recipient please come forward and claim his property."

Mr. Bruce cleared his throat. "This letter, I should add, has a very imaginatively decorated envelope. It's full of hearts and Xs and Os and, best of all, on the back, there's a large pair of lipstick lips."

He held up the envelope. A wave of laughter filled the mess hall.

Mr. Bruce put on his reading glasses. "'Dear Ted,'" he began, "'why haven't you written? Things have been so dull here at Camp Loraine since the dance.'"

Ted was outraged. He knew now who this letter was from and why it was being read.

Mr. Bruce continued. " 'I miss you. I miss holding your hand and talking. . . .'"

The whole camp hooted.

Ted grabbed the letter. "You've stolen this out of the mail," he shouted into the microphone. "You and Jack Dunn are guilty of mail theft and mail tampering. You could go to jail."

"Wait a minute, Ted," said Mr. Bruce. "I'm sorry you're upset. This was just meant to be a—"

"I know what it was meant to be. We don't have to look any further than Jack Dunn for that."

The camp was in an uproar. People were standing and shouting or whispering among themselves. Suddenly everyone was quiet.

Jack Dunn stood in the aisle. "Ted," he said, "I think you owe Mr. Bruce and me an apology."

"Apology!" said Ted. "After what you've done?"

"And what exactly did we do?"

"You heard me!"

"I think you exaggerated a little."

Jack had orchestrated this humiliating moment. And now, in front of everyone, he was trying to bargain it away!

Jack saw him coming and stood his ground. Ted slammed into him and knocked him sprawling.

Counselors appeared. They grabbed Ted by the arms and pulled him backwards. Jack tried to lunge but was held fast.

"Let me finish the creep!" he shouted.

A hush had fallen over the mess hall. People sat where they were, not quite able to figure out what had happened. Was Jack really responsible for the letter prank? Was this enough to cause a fight?

Surrounded by counselors, Ted was led back to the microphone and his cake. Mr. Bruce came up to him.

"Ted, I'm sorry. I had no idea you would be so upset. Jack thought, well, he found the letter and—oh, come on and have a piece of cake. Then you can bring the rest back to your table."

So it *had* been Jack. And Mr. Bruce didn't know what was going on between Jack and Ted.

The piece of cake was large and square. Moist devil's food with a creamy white icing. He bit into it. What should have been sweet and delicious tasted like sawdust. Over his shoulder he noticed Jack Dunn storm out of the mess hall.

Fifteen

"Did you see Jack's face when he left?"

"I was too far away."

"White as a ghost."

It was later that night. The rain had stopped, leaving the air damp and chilly but clear. Ted and Lee were hanging out on the porch of the administration building. They'd gone to canteen and bought nothing. Too much birthday cake.

"I'm not surprised," said Ted.

"What do you think he'll try now?"

"I don't know. But I think we should do something first."

"Us?"

Ted was sitting on the porch rail. He looked over his shoulder. "I don't see anyone else around."

"You're serious, of course."

"As serious as Jack."

"I had the feeling you might say that."

"You've got cold feet."

"Me? Never. Feel."

Lee scrunched down in his wicker chair. He held out a booted foot.

Ted laughed. "Really, we can't just let Jack alone. Whatever he does next is going to be awful."

"What can we do?"

"We've got a haunted-house trip coming up next week. That's the time."

"Will I be able to handle this?"

"I hope so. When Jack and Ricky go for me, you're coming in to help."

"Oh, my God. We're capturing the ghosts."

"Yes. Sort of."

"What good will it do?"

"I'm not sure exactly. But at least a whole bunch of Horsemen will know what's going on. Anyway, it's the best plan I can come up with at the moment. I just wish Ricky didn't enjoy being as vicious as his brother. I'd rather go one on one with Jack."

"You know how much Ricky idolizes Jack. He'd do anything Jack told him and enjoy it, too. But people seem to like getting scared at these damn houses. They like it as much as the riding."

"I don't think they like getting creamed. They're just too scared to admit it."

"And Mr. Bruce?"

"Once he knows what Jack's really up to, he'll have to do something."

"You hope."

"I wish. My feet are colder than yours."

The following Tuesday, Cabin 3, Horseman Division, was called for a haunted-house trip. With them would be Cabins 1 and 5. Unfortunately, Cabin 5's best-known occupant was chubby, whiny Richie Clark.

Richie had been thrown in the watering trough three

times in the last two weeks. Not that Ted was concerned. Richie Clark was so obnoxious—so ready to complain and disagree about everything—that Ted would have been glad to see him dunked daily. And though Ted reproached himself for his lack of charity, he secretly wished the kid had gone on an earlier one of these trips and been coaxed into the house. Richie Clark in a potato sack was not an unwelcome prospect.

Of course, it never would have happened. Nothing could have brought Richie close to the house, much less into it. As they all piled into the GMC, he was already shaking like a leaf.

Sitting next to Lee, Mr. Bruce's neck and head looming in front, Ted had an odd sense of déjà vu. There, all lit up, were the administration building and the canteen. Just down from them was the mess hall, in darkness, where Jack would be assembling his crew. They would watch T. R. drive off, just as he had watched when he had done the haunting. He and Tim were in the GMC. Who would be taking their places?

Before they'd gone a mile, Richie Clark squealed, "Are we stopping for a snack?"

"Of course, Richie," said Mr. Bruce. "The choice is between the Moonglow Diner in town and the Dairy Queen on the highway."

There was some discussion of where to go. The diner won easily.

"Good choice," said Mr. Bruce. "Best chocolate milkshakes in the state."

The GMC was bulky and squat, but the way T. R. drove it, it became more like him: long, sleek, a little sinister. In

126

no time at all they had reached the town and pulled into the diner's parking lot.

Getting out, standing in the cold air, Ted felt the night envelop them. He battled against his fear, but it wouldn't go away.

The diner was long and narrow, with aluminum sides. The perfect, traditional, oversized, railroad dining car. On the top was a huge neon sign, advertising to at least three states: MOONGLOW DINER.

Only there was no moon. And no more than the slightest hint of one behind the clouds.

The boys huddled together in the red leatherette booths. They ordered milkshakes and Cokes and hamburgers. Somebody had a piece of blueberry pie. T. R. Bruce presided over it all, sounding warm, friendly, and elated.

Ted could barely drink his milkshake, barely touch his hamburger. The light in the place was too bright, the stainless steel of the counter and stools, too shiny. The whiteness of the tile floor made him dizzy. He looked across at Lee, who had ordered a Coke and drunk only half. They smiled grim, conspiratorial smiles at one another.

No one had anything to say. No one finished his food.

Mr. Bruce looked at his watch. "Time to leave."

He paid the check with a flourish. They all scrambled out to the GMC and were in darkness once again.

Driving along, the gloom seemed even greater than before. This time Ted was sitting next to Richie Clark. Richie was gripping the seat in front of him so hard, his knuckles had turned white.

"By the way," Mr. Bruce said, "tonight we're going to the Bigelow house. For those of you who haven't been, the

127

Bigelows were shot dead in their living room about a dozen years ago. Nobody's been in the house since, except us."

A gasp from Richie Clark, who was now trembling so hard, he seemed like a windup toy let loose. Everyone else looked stonily ahead.

The thing about these trips, Ted realized, was that no matter how often you went, they always got to you. There were guys in this group who had been to haunted houses half a dozen times. They didn't look any happier than the ones who'd never been before.

"Was the murderer ever caught?" he asked.

"Why, no," said Mr. Bruce. "In fact, some people say he's been seen lurking around the house the last few weeks."

"They know who did it?"

"Yes, but knowing hasn't made him easier to catch. It was their son, John."

The first name made the idea of the murder that much more real. Ted glanced at Lee, who looked grim, then over at Hambone, who drew a finger across his throat and leered. Tim was looking out the window, obviously paying no attention. He knew what was likely to happen at this house. And none of it would happen to him. But Hambone? Ted couldn't tell if he was scared or not. He'd been to the houses, he knew about Jack, but was that enough if you hadn't worked inside?

The GMC was off the hardtop now and bouncing along a dirt road through some woods.

"This house is quite deep in the woods," said Mr. Bruce. "We'll walk from the bottom of the driveway."

A moment later they pulled off the road and stopped. Mr. Bruce cleared his throat. "Someone has to guard the car. You lock the doors and roll up the windows. It's worth a B − ."

"I'll do it!" said Richie Clark.

Mr. Bruce turned. On his face was a look of such contempt, it seemed to sum up all his feelings about the importance of these expeditions and what did and did not make a Cherokee camper.

"That's just fine, Richie," he said. "You've solved our problem for us. If anything goes wrong, just sound the horn."

Everyone else piled out into the road. As they started down the driveway through the woods, Ted looked back. Richie was locking doors and closing windows. He looked like a monkey in a glassed-in cage.

The woods were very dark and dense. Their flashlight beams bobbed along the drive, providing all that there was of warmth and safety. These beams, Ted knew, would tip off Jack and his friends that they were coming.

There was a bend in the drive. Once around it, they could no longer see the car. For better or worse, Richie Clark was now completely alone.

They stopped about fifty yards from the house. It was, Ted could see, much smaller than the Wilson house. A two-story Cape Cod box, it looked as if someone had beaten it around the midsection and then tried to straighten it up again.

Because it was small, there couldn't be many places to hide.

"Okay," said Mr. Bruce, sounding impatient to get started. "Most of you know the rules. The rest will know them soon enough. Who's going first?"

"I'll go," Tim said.

129

"Timmy," said Mr. Bruce. "A real sport."

"I'm going inside," said Tim.

Everyone followed his back as he walked up to the house, knocked on the door, asked the ritual "Can we camp here for the night?" and went in. There was some scuffling—or what sounded like it—the slamming of a door, and some rocks flying out a window. Ted smiled when he heard the rocks. Then there was Tim's light shining through the top front window.

Of course. They'd let him through.

Everyone cheered.

A moment later Tim was back, smiling and triumphant. "Nice B+ work," said Mr. Bruce, patting him on the shoulder.

"It wasn't bad," said Tim, "but it sure was weird. All that slamming around. I wonder who's in the place? I hope it's not John."

Ted couldn't believe what a hypocrite Tim was. He said, "I'll go next."

Mr. Bruce glanced over. "Good for you, Ted. I'm glad to see you've got guts."

"I'm going for a B+."

Someone took a deep breath. Maybe he'd done it himself.

"We all wish you good luck," said Mr. Bruce.

"Yeah," said Hambone. "Good luck, Ted."

"Yeah, good luck," said Tim.

Yeah, sure, thought Ted. Good luck and a bullet in the back.

He started down the rest of the driveway. The woods closed in on him from either side. Halfway to the house, he heard some rustling on his left, then a low, very human growl. He wondered who it might be but paid no attention.

No rocks cascaded down as he reached the house. Someone was not at the switch. He climbed the porch steps, went through the "Can we camp here for the night?" ritual, and opened the front door.

He was standing in the entrance hall. To his left was the stairway; to his right, what was obviously the living room. For some reason, knowing he shouldn't be wasting time, he poked his flashlight into the living room first.

His blood froze. On the floor, between the sofa and a wing chair, were two bodies with a sheet thrown over them!

This had to be a joke. He stepped forward. The bodies were dummies. He left the living room for the stairs, trembling slightly.

Shining his light up ahead of him, he noticed what he hadn't noticed before. At the top of the stairs was a door.

He was looking around at the ugly green wallpaper, wondering how to negotiate this new development, when the door opened and something came flying out. It struck him in the chest and bounced off. He jumped back, more shocked than frightened.

It took a moment to pull himself together. Then he trained his flashlight on the object that had struck him. A dead mouse.

"All right, Jack!" Ted shouted. "Enough's enough. I'm coming for you now."

He started up the stairs. Was he crazy? Announcing himself in this way? Jack wasn't going to be alone up there. Ricky would be with him, and God knows who else might join in. Would there be enough of a commotion? Would Lee, and anyone else for that matter, get to him in time?

Three steps from the top, the door opened again. More objects came flying out. Ted lurched back, bracing himself against the wall.

He didn't have to shine his light on what had hit him this time. Horse turds had a special quality all their own.

"Jack," Ted shouted, "do you eat it, too?"

No reply. But the door opened and a whole barrage of rocks flew down the stairs.

Ted was still leaning against the wall. They missed him, but he was getting angry.

He climbed to the top step and tried the door. It wouldn't budge. He banged on it and said, "What's the matter, Jack? Lost your nerve?"

There was laughter on the other side. It sounded like Jack and Ricky.

He banged on the door again. "Come on," he said, "don't you want some fun? I'm here for a B+, remember?"

The laughter grew louder. Then a low voice said, "We're so far ahead of you. Do you really think we'd let you trap us?"

"What do you mean?" Ted said.

"Just remember. We've got your number."

"Bastard," said Ted under his breath.

Suddenly there was chaos outside, the car horn beeping wildly, the sound of voices and running feet in the driveway. Richie Clark had lost his cool. This trip was over.

Sixteen

The next day was warm and sunny. Having slept out in a field with the rest of the group and come back to camp just in time to pick up their horses from the pasture, Ted and Lee were only too glad to finish their hour of riding, skip individual activity (with permission), and get to the waterfront for a swim.

"Gee, you must love me a lot," said Monty Benson when he'd heard they planned to spend the rest of the morning at the lake.

"Yeah," said Ted, "it's your pretty face."

"Nah," said Lee, "it's your ugly feet."

"No kidding," said Monty, looking down. "You really love me for my feet? That's something."

"Sure," said Lee. "Can we take out a canoe the first hour? Before we have our class?"

"But you'll be so far away," said Monty. "That doesn't sound like love to me."

"We'll love you from afar," said Ted.

"In that case, how could I refuse? A guy who loves you for your feet from afar can't be all bad."

They took a quick dip to get the dust and grime off. Then away.

The canoe glided through the water, Ted in front and

Lee behind. Monty, Ted realized, had never so much as asked what happened on the Old Glory Road. But Monty was hardly the sort who would.

They stopped paddling. Ted turned around. The canoe floated happily, water clunking against its sides. Far off there was a splash followed by a whistle.

"At last, privacy," said Ted.

"Yeah," said Lee. "Or do you think Jack's got the lake wired for sound?"

"God, how I hated him talking to me through that door."

"It's about as exasperating as Richie Clark messing up the whole plan for nothing."

"You think he didn't see anybody at all?"

"There was somebody in the woods all right—"

"I know that. I heard him, too."

"But he wasn't anywhere near the GMC."

"Didn't you love the way T. R. made Richie sleep in the GMC? So he wouldn't be scared?"

"Except," said Lee, "I wasn't so wild about sleeping on the ground either. Without a tent, in the middle of that field, it was freezing."

He leaned back in the canoe. "At least it's warm today. That sun's baking my bones."

"Mine, too," said Ted. "I just wish Jack weren't so interested in *breaking* my bones."

"Any thoughts about what to do next?"

"None. Everything Jack does, he does in the middle of some weird camp event. It's always beyond the limit, but he knows no one's going to risk being called a coward and complain. If he can go after you with a cattle prod and get away with it, just think what he must have planned for me."

"So you're going to be a sitting duck."

"Unless *you've* got any bright ideas."

"Fresh out. You think he'll try something Parents' Weekend?"

"Who knows?"

Lee trailed his hand in the water. "It's just bad all around."

That afternoon, it was as if everyone realized for the first time that Parents' Weekend existed. At lunch Mr. Bruce made an announcement that after rest hour there would be no afternoon activity. All campers were to return to their individual activities and start preparing whatever it was they had to prepare for Saturday morning. The Horsemen, on the other hand, would go straight to the barn for extra tack cleaning. As the groan went up, Mr. Bruce raised his hand and said, "Don't we want to look our best for the show Sunday?"

"Yes," came the reply, forty voices as one.

"Then drop your cocks and grab your socks," said Mr. Bruce.

The Horsemen laughed—and went to the barn after rest hour. Lee brought his saddle and bridle over to Nelly's stall.

They were just finishing when Jack came around a corner with a pitchfork. He stopped and stood there—dark, menacing. Then he stuck the pitchfork in a post and walked away.

The next couple of days were a whirlwind of activity. Riding lessons were all preparations for the show. The Horsemen set up ropes around the edge of the riding field, defining a quarter-mile track. On that track, late Sunday

135

afternoon, the race known as the Cherokee Sweepstakes would be run. Down at the waterfront, Monty Benson and his crew were busy preparing demonstrations on every level. At all the individual activities, wondrous things were being completed. Ted was a little embarrassed by his traditional lanyard and ashtray at arts and crafts and secretly wished he'd stuck with riflery and could display his prowess on the range. But Lee had made a terrific chief's headdress at Indian lore and was very proud.

By Friday Jack had still not played his hand.

"Do you think he's backed off?" Lee asked at lunch.

Ted grimaced. "I wouldn't count on it."

In the afternoon he went to the stable for a rehearsal of the Horsemen's special annual Friday evening performance. It was, he had to admit, another of those weird Cherokee events and therefore fair game for a Jack Dunn surprise. On the other hand, it was a rehearsal and full of people. What could Jack do?

Ted had been chosen to perform in the event. Lee, of course, had not.

Higg had left a large carton in the middle of the yard. On closer inspection, it turned out to be filled with musty, old Indian costumes. The ten Horsemen selected—Tim was there, along with Jack, Mike Schroeder, and six others— had to choose their costumes from the box.

"When you're dressed," Higg said, pulling on his pipe, "ride your horses bareback to the riding field. We'll go on from there."

Ten people descended on the box, pulling out this pair of pants and that fancy headdress. After a moment, Ted realized it wasn't worth the struggle. He waited until everyone had chosen, then pulled out a loincloth, a beaded headband with two feathers, and a vest with lots of fringe. As he held up the vest for a closer look, he discovered someone else's hand on it.

"You'd better let me have the vest," said Jack.

It wasn't even a great vest! Was he going to make an issue of this? Right here? Right now? He let his hand slip away.

Ted got himself under control. He found an old buckskin jacket with a hole in one elbow. It would do well enough.

He changed into his costume, complete with the moccasins he'd brought from the cabin, in Nelly's stall. Then he bridled Nelly, led her out into the yard, and mounted up.

He loved gripping her sides with his bare legs. As long as she didn't trot and bounce him up and down, he was fine. But how was she going to take what was coming up?

At the edge of the riding field, the ten Indians gathered in a line. They faced a beaten-up covered wagon, languishing at the bottom of the hill. The wagon was filled with hay.

Each of the Indians was handed a lighted torch the length of a lance and the width of a husky broomstick. Smoke from kerosene-soaked rags burning on one end filled the air.

Nelly was already skittish from the smoke and flame. When Higg yelled "Charge!" and the other horses took off, she reared and followed them. Riding bareback in his loincloth, it was all Ted could do to hang on, first when she was in the air and next as she catapulted down the hill.

He recovered quickly enough to hurl his torch into the covered wagon and stop Nelly before she hit the hardtop road. Not everyone was so lucky. Mike Schroeder and Jim Burns fell off and had to be helped back on their horses.

"Shit, this is fun!" Jack yelled as they started up the hill to try once more. He looked like a renegade chief in the vest and a fabulous headdress that ran halfway down his back.

"Okay," Higg said when they had reassembled, "stay a little closer together and try to throw the torches at the same time. Remember, you've got to control your horses."

Already the hay was burning brightly. They would help it burn some more. Doug Parelli and Hank French, another riding counselor, picked up the torches on foot and brought them to the Indians.

The second time down, Jack was side by side with Ted. They were together—whooping it up like crazy—until they reached the wagon. As Ted raised his arm to throw the torch, he got a glimpse of Jack's maniacal grin. He threw, then ducked as Jack's torch flew past his ear. Both struck their mark, and Jack pulled Big Red away, laughing wildly.

Ted was so shaken, he took a moment to recover himself, letting Nelly stand quietly at the bottom of the hill. He leaned forward, arms around her neck. Then he urged her slowly back up to the others.

Of course no one had seen. But then, what had there been to see?

"We'll do this one more time," said Higg. "You looked much better, and no one fell off. I think you'll do fine tonight. Hold your costumes till after the performance. Remember, we meet for makeup at eight-thirty and start at nine."

The last time down, Ted made sure he was nowhere near

Jack. He threw his torch, stopped Nelly, then jumped off and led her across the road to the barn.

He watered her and put her in her stall. He changed back into his jeans and boots, bundled up the costume and hid it at the bottom of the manger. Then he leaned his head against his horse's side.

Nelly shifted her weight and moved over slightly. Ted reached forward and patted her nose as she bent to munch some hay. He left the stall and entered the yard, intending to start back up the hill.

Over by the watering trough lay the torches, cold and smoldering. Beside them was a can of kerosene and—incredibly—a box of kitchen matches. As Ted watched, horrified, Jack Dunn appeared, doused one of the torches in kerosene, and lit it.

Everyone else had gone. As Jack started toward him, blazing torch in hand, Ted found himself evaluating the possibilities. Both wearing jeans and engineer boots. Both tall and pretty fast. He took off across the yard.

With a shout, Jack went after him. But Ted had a head start. And he didn't have a lighted torch to carry. Within a few strides, Jack was yards behind. With a yelp of frustration, he hurled the torch at Ted.

Hearing it hit the ground, Ted stopped running. He faced Jack.

"Okay, smartass," he said. "Now you can take me on, fair and square."

But Jack wasn't having any. He ducked into the tool shed and came out with a pitchfork.

Ted danced away. "So this is the way you fight fair, Jack. I've never seen such courage."

Jack lunged at Ted with the pitchfork. Ted backed into the tool shed. As Jack lunged again, Ted parried with a rake.

Ted maneuvered himself around the shed, hoping to escape. But there wasn't enough space to move Jack out of position. Each time he lunged at Ted, he jumped back to block the door.

"Jack," Ted said, "if you jab me with that pitchfork, how will you explain it away? You've got no cover on this one."

Jack's face twisted into a knot of rage. He rushed at Ted, pitchfork level with his chest. Ted darted to the right, slipped and fell to the floor. Jack was on him, and raised the pitchfork high.

This is it, thought Ted. It's all over.

But the pitchfork never fell. Suddenly Lee was there, wrestling with Jack. Jack pushed Lee away. He got the pitchfork back and stood up.

But Ted was ready for him now. He swung the rake and hit Jack in the side. The pitchfork popped out of his hands and clattered to the floor.

"Ow!" said Jack, like a small boy who's been hurt.

Then he realized where he was and ran for the door.

"You bastards!" he shouted over his shoulder. "You wait!"

Seventeen

After they had recovered their wits, Ted asked Lee how he'd managed to arrive when he did.

"I left Indian lore early," Lee said. "I got worried."

"You saved my life."

"Just like you saved mine."

It was after dinner now. The campers were waiting in their cabins for their parents. Everyone was getting nervous. The parents would reveal more about the campers than the campers had ever revealed about themselves.

As he waited, Ted thought about that moment in the tool shed and tried to convince himself that he and Lee would escape Jack's wrath and somehow bring him down. He was still trying to convince himself of this when Tim's mother appeared.

She was trim and pretty, with auburn hair, gold earrings, and a pert little nose like Tim's. She smiled easily when introduced, but after that her only interest was the contents of Tim's trunk. She'd brought him some new riding clothes, but she hadn't brought a thing for the bunk. Hambone, Lee, and Ted were getting quite uncomfortable when Hambone's parents arrived.

Hambone's father was a large man with skinny arms and legs, a lot of white hair, and pale eyes. His mother was little and plump, with short curly hair and a puckish grin. After they had embraced Hambone and been introduced, Hambone's father said, "Okay now, here are the goodies. We know you guys never get anything decent to eat."

Out came potato chips and Doritos, peanut-butter crackers and Oreos, Twinkies and Tastykakes. And even though it was just after dinner, everyone dug in.

In the middle of all this gluttony, there was a knock on the door. Lee's parents weren't coming—they were on a trip to Greece—so it had to be Ted's.

Suddenly Ted was overcome by homesickness. He missed their friendly, cavernous apartment, his father's earnest enthusiasm, his mother's gentle good humor. He wanted to tell them everything, to have them take him away or stop Jack or both. But he knew he wouldn't tell them anything, that they had no part to play here, except as guests.

And then there they were, hugging him, and he was just so glad to see them, none of the rest of it mattered.

His father was tall and lean, with short salt-and-pepper hair and horn-rimmed glasses. His mother was dark blonde and sort of preppy, with a straight nose and bangs. He introduced them around, and they were polite and cheerful to everyone.

After a moment, they pulled out their own goodies: sunflower seeds, unsalted peanuts, raisins, apricots, zucchini bread, natural cheddar cheese, sesame crackers.

"It's the health-food nuts against the junk-food addicts," said Hambone's father.

"We love junk food, too," said Ted's mother. "Why don't we all share?"

And they did. Even Tim's mother grew less pissy. And then it was time for the Friday evening performance.

It came off without a hitch. In war paint and shouting, they swarmed down the hill, their torches lighting up the darkness, the hapless covered wagon bursting into flame once more. Gathered across the road, the rest of the campers and their parents oohed and aahed and applauded as the Indians vanished into the barn. Who cared about fire and destruction? These boys were at a camp that specialized in rugged, daredevil stuff. It was the perfect way to kick off Parents' Weekend.

During the Saturday exhibitions, which seemed to go by in a flash, parents kept coming up and congratulating Ted on his performance as an Indian the night before. No wonder Jack got away with everything. If the parents didn't consider torching a covered wagon barbaric and kept coming back to see it burn year after year, why would anyone else object to such behavior? And if T. R. Bruce or Jack Dunn did some odd things a little too oddly, well, that was all part of it. Wasn't it? Even if the parents knew the details of these odd things, most of them probably wouldn't complain.

Coming back from Indian lore, where Lee's headdress had been a great hit, Ted's mother said, "Lee, I hope you'll join us for dinner."

"Yes," said Ted's father in his familiar courtly style, "we'd be honored."

Lee looked at Ted, who threw up his hands.

"Thank you," Lee said. "I accept."

They were allowed to be out until ten. They had to wear their uniforms. They went to Romano's, the best pizza place in town.

It was in a small, white, clapboard house, with a gracious front room and a porch for drinking. They sat inside at a round table with a red-checked cloth and a dripping candle in the middle. Mrs. Romano herself—a large, sunny lady in a soiled white apron—came and took their order. Two large, one sausage and mushroom, one pepperoni. Two Lite beers. Two Cokes.

The pizzas came, large, bubbling platters.

"Mmm," said Ted's mother. "I haven't had such good pizza anywhere in New York."

"It's something about the crust," said Ted's father. "Not so doughy."

Ted had to smile. His parents could be enthusiastic about anything.

"Tell us about your summer," said his mother. "We want to hear everything about everything that hasn't been in your letters."

Well, let me see, Ted thought to himself. He'd just missed getting impaled on a pitchfork, Lee was practically branded with a cattle prod, and at the haunted houses. . . No, they didn't want to hear everything about everything. And even if they did and they believed him, they'd only want to take him home. That wouldn't help him get Jack.

"The riding's been great," Ted said. "I've made a lot of progress with Nelly, and the overnight trip I went on was a lot of fun. The other day we went canoeing by ourselves, and it was so peaceful and quiet. . . ."

The conversation dipped and spun. Suddenly, in the middle, Ted heard Lee say, "And there was Old Glory Road Night."

"What's Old Glory Road Night?" Ted's father asked.

"You remember, Dad," said Ted. "I wrote you both about it."

"Oh, yes," said Ted's father. "I remember now. It sounded scary, but it must have been fun, too."

"Oh, yes," said Lee. "Lots of fun."

The conversation whirled on, touching here and there, always avoiding the curious or the dangerously suggestive remark. Lee didn't slip again.

Finally Ted's mother stretched, looked at her watch, and said, "Well, gang, time for your beauty sleep."

The pizzas were long gone. There had been more beer and more Cokes.

"I don't know about you," said Ted's father, "but I need to walk off some of this food. Then we'll get you back."

They walked through town. The main street was closed up tight. All the houses were dark.

Ted's father kept his hands clasped behind his back. "You know," he said, "you guys are really lucky. It's so peaceful here, so totally removed from what life is like in the city. It's almost like not being part of the modern world. Camping out. Looking after the horses. It must be easy to have a good time."

Ted glanced at Lee and tried not to laugh. "Oh, sure," he said. "The horses are great, and you make good friends, too."

"And the tradition Mr. Bruce keeps talking about. All those old-fashioned, honest virtues and the boys coming back year after year. Doesn't it make you feel good to be part of something like that?"

This time the laughter bubbled up and out. Ted had to hold a hand over his mouth to stop it.

Ted's father stared at him. "I don't understand. What was so funny?"

Ted touched his father's arm. "It's okay, Dad, really, it's okay. Mr. Bruce's traditions are great. It's just"—he glanced again at Lee—"it's just a private joke."

The rest of the walk was quiet. When they got back to the car, Ted's mother said, "I don't know how you boys do it. Six A.M. every day. I don't think I'd make it."

"Sometimes I wonder myself," Ted said.

Back in camp, sitting on the edge of his bunk, he whispered good night to Lee.

"Hey, Ted," Lee said.

"Yuh?"

"I really enjoyed being with your parents."

"That's good. We enjoyed having you."

"I'm sorry I mentioned the road. It was dumb."

"It's okay. I'm sorry I laughed at my dad. Get some sleep now."

"Okay. You, too."

But he couldn't. He lay on his bed in his clothes, hoping to relax. Every time he closed his eyes, his thoughts sneaked up on him. Maybe he should have told his parents. Maybe they could have done something.

He got up and tiptoed outside. Some air might clear his head.

He sat on the cabin steps and took a few deep breaths. They didn't do any good. A light was on in Higg's cabin down the row. He remembered what Lee had told him about Higg. But he also remembered the way Higg had looked at Jack on the overnight. He had to talk to someone.

Higg was just taking off his boots when Ted crept through the door. He squinted to see who it was, then placed a finger over his lips.

Ted sat down on the bed.

"What's going on?" Higg whispered.

"I'm not sure," Ted said, in a voice so low it was almost inaudible. "I'm not sure if I can even tell you."

Higg reached for his pipe. "If you've got something to tell me, tell me."

"It's about Jack."

"Jack?"

"He's trying to kill me."

He knew it was too strong the moment he said it. Anything he said next was going to sound like an exaggeration. He said it anyway. All of it.

When he was through, Higg leaned forward. The dim light reflected off his sharp features.

"Look, Ted," he said. "Jack may be too impetuous sometimes, and you know I don't approve of that. But couldn't you be overreacting a little?"

"The cattle prod and the pitchfork made themselves very clear, sir."

Higg shook his head. "Jack is respected here. We're an unusual kind of place, and he's part of it. So are you now. What you describe sounds like a foolish quarrel. Can't the two of you talk it out?"

"No, sir. I don't think we can."

He rose to leave. "Thank you for listening." He held out his hand.

Higg took it. "After the show, you and Jack should get together. If you like, I'll join you."

"That would be fine."

Higg patted Ted on the shoulder. "Good luck tomorrow. I'm counting on you for some ribbons."

"Thanks. I'll need all the luck I can find."

It was hopeless. A nice man, but Lee had his number. He kicked a stone as he walked back to his cabin.

Wait. He had one more shot. He crept into the cabin and crouched by Hambone's bed.

Ted shook him lightly. Hambone mumbled something unintelligible and turned over on his stomach.

Ted shook him again. Hambone opened one eye. "What is it, Ted?"

"It's about Jack."

"Jack? It's the middle of the night!"

"He tried to stab me with a pitchfork."

Hambone buried his head in his pillow.

"Are you going to help me?"

"Man," said Hambone, "if there was something I could do for you, I'd do it, but right now what I need is some sleep. Tomorrow's a long day."

"Sorry I woke you," said Ted.

He got back on his bunk, stretched out, and placed his hands behind his head. He didn't need to sleep to know he was in the middle of a nightmare.

Eighteen

The parade began at the stable at nine. Dressed in breeches and their green shirts and green and gold ties, forty Horsemen lined up in a column of twos behind Higg on Jericho. Jack was up ahead, near Lee on Flash. Ted was toward the rear on Nelly.

It had rained heavily during the night, a Cherokee horse show tradition. The two rings would be muddy now, the track surrounding them a slippery, sodden mess. A light mist still hung in the air, helping to chill the bones. Usually it burned off by eleven. Today, because there was no sun, it would linger.

Hooves clattering across the hardtop, forty horses started up the Old Glory Road. Sitting erect in the saddle, Higg looked every inch the regal riding master. And forty Horsemen, swelling their chests, arching their backs, holding their reins just so, tried to look as good.

There was no music, but there might as well have been. Campers and parents lined the road applauding, and as the horses turned off toward the corral, everyone cheered.

Ted was wearing his new black boots with the brown hunting tops. They gleamed. So did Nelly's tack and Nelly herself. He'd been grooming her for an hour and was proud

149

of them both. It didn't even matter how soggy they got later on.

Fears still prowling the back of his mind, he'd plunged into the occasion. The parade looked beautiful. Everyone was excited. He was going to win some ribbons. How could he not feel a thrill?

Besides, he had too much to do to worry. With the horses tied up in the corral, it was time for the first class: Junior Equitation. And just as they would all morning, the Horsemen got everyone mounted and ready.

Girth checked. Stirrups shortened. Out into the ring past throngs of parents hugging the rail.

During the classes, he watched with Lee. How impressive it all seemed. Two professional judges, Mr. and Mrs. Rogers, had been brought in. They wore identical red jackets, white breeches, and black boots. Tall and blond, their hair only just visible beneath their black hunting caps, each ruled a ring. And round and round them went the horses, all trying to obey the commands.

Trot, please. Canter, please. Walk, please. Half-turn, please. Change hands, please. Ted laughed delightedly when an Intermediate boy won third place on Nelly. She was still hard to handle, and others riding her hadn't done so well.

When he'd stopped laughing, Lee asked, "Is everything okay?"

For a second, he was too bound up in the moment to understand. "Oh," he said, "I have no idea."

And he didn't. He'd hardly seen Jack all morning. He knew he must be helping out somewhere but wasn't sure where. Let him stay as far away as he pleased.

The last event of the morning was the Hunt Class for Horsemen. As he rode into the ring, he saw his parents sitting on folding chairs on the far side. He waved. They waved back.

What a lift that gave him. All forty Horsemen performed in the opening, equitation part of the class. He executed so well he knew he'd made the finals before his name was announced. Best of all, Lee had made them, too!

So there, Higg! So there's the rider you wouldn't choose for your polo team!

The seven finalists had to jump two railroad-tie jumps on the riding field, then a chicken coop that took them into the woods and over a short hunt course built years ago by Horsemen themselves. The course was treacherous at best, and in this kind of damp weather it could be hell. Ted figured he was probably second to Tim at this point. If he could pull off a perfect round now, he could win.

He almost did. He cleared the two railroad ties flawlessly, went over the chicken coop, the first stone wall, and the in-and-out. The in-and-out was always the toughest, and, once he was past it, he relaxed a little. He shouldn't have. Coming into the brush jump, a little shaky on the wet ground, Nelly ticked one of the logs. It fell, and he was second.

Behind Tim, of course. But Lee was third! Didn't a second and a third together add up to more than a first? As they gathered in a line in the ring to receive their ribbons, his parents cheering in the background, he hugged Lee hard.

Then he leaned over to Tim, who was looking straight ahead, waiting for the picture to be snapped. The blue, red, gold, and white ribbons hung from the horses' bridles. As

T. R. Bruce clicked the shutter, Ted grabbed Tim's hand. Tim looked as if he'd just been goosed by an ice pick.

Taking Nelly down to the barn before lunch, Ted savored the congratulations of his parents and the other Horsemen. He also savored his red ribbon, the first horse-show ribbon he had ever won. There was something classy about its silky shine.

But there was no time to dwell on these things. After lunch, following Senior Equitation, the Cherokee Sweepstakes were coming right up.

Eight horses had been chosen for the race. Nelly was among them. At lunch there was a drawing. Each of eight lucky parents got a horse to bet on. Was anyone concerned that the track was really too small for a race or that the slick, muddy surface from the previous night's rain had made it dangerous? No. Everyone wanted to win.

It was only during rest hour that Ted began to feel nervous. His stomach churned. His hands were like ice.

Saddling up for the afternoon, he asked Lee how he felt about the track.

"So it's risky," said Lee. "Go for it!"

"I wish you'd been chosen, too."

"Win for both of us."

By post time he'd pulled himself together. Jack had seized the pole position. Jim Burns and Mike Schroeder were beside him. Tim, on Tar Baby, was in the middle of the pack. Somehow, through no fault of his own, Ted had ended up on the outside. It wasn't going to matter. Nelly would blow them all away.

He held her in, the reins tight in his hands, waiting for the gun.

"Everyone into line, please," Higg said, as a few of the horses danced restlessly about. He raised the starting gun over his head.

It went off, sounding so loud in Ted's ears he thought he had gone deaf. As it sounded, Nelly shied to the right.

He pulled her back onto the track and let her loose, then held her in again as they plowed through the first turn, running next to last.

The ground was so slippery, it was hard to keep control. Huge chunks of mud flew back in his face, splattered him, Nelly, the saddle. It didn't matter, as long as he could see through the mist.

He picked up ground on the second straightaway. Nelly seemed to be finding her stride. Slithering out of the second turn, hearing the wet slogging of the hooves, he was fifth.

Once more around!

He let Nelly fly down the straightaway, knowing he couldn't hold her back on the turn. He couldn't afford to lose any ground.

He found a place along the rail, gripped hard with his thighs, buried his face in Nelly's mane. Ahead, Jim Burns was doing the same thing. But Dusty was too much for him, and the track was too slick. He couldn't keep her in the turn. Suddenly she slid wide to the right and piled into the ropes.

All Ted could see as he flew by was a panicked horse with an empty saddle.

He shot out of the turn, going so fast everything was a blur. Fifteen yards in front, three horses were bunched together. Big Red was a neck ahead on the inside, but Tim on Tar Baby and Mike Schroeder on Princess were gaining.

For the first time in the race, Ted kicked Nelly. "Come on, Nell! Come on, babe!"

And she responded. Going into the last turn, she pulled to within inches of Tar Baby and Princess. Somehow, coming out of the turn, she squeezed in beside Big Red.

Four horses plunged toward the finish line. Four horses straining for their best through mist and mud.

They flew down the stretch, and Ted urged Nelly one more time. She moved ahead by an inch, ahead by half a neck. She was going to win!

Jack kicked Big Red as hard as he could. He hit him with his crop.

But Big Red lost another inch. Cursing, Jack struck Ted across the face with the crop.

The pain nearly blinded him at first, a solid block of numbness mixed with sparks. He reached for his eyes, and, as he reached, he fell.

He lost the reins, bounced off Big Red's side. And there was the ground. Mud, stones, pounding hooves, and then nothing.

Nineteen

He woke up in the infirmary. A bandage covered the left side of his head. There were cuts on his face and bruises all over his body. The crisp sheets, the firm bed, the whiteness of everything soothed him. But nothing could contain his anger.

Lee was beside him.

"Jack did this!" Ted said.

"I saw," said Lee. "I was at the rail."

"It was just what he wanted. So much confusion. All that flying mud. The perfect moment. Nobody else would have seen."

"And he won the race."

"Of course. The son of a bitch."

Ted pounded his hand into the pillow. "I had him beat. I could taste it."

"I know. But this is Jack we're talking about. Remember? Jack, who wanted to kill you? Be grateful it wasn't worse."

"Has anyone said how serious it is?"

"No. But your parents are talking to the doctor now. You didn't look so great when they scooped you out of the mud."

"You *sound* so serious, though. You think Jack's got more coming?"

"I think he's through with you. He must have gotten a

real charge out of dumping you in front of all those people and making it look like your fault."

"That's for sure."

"I think he'll be after me."

There was silence in the room. Ted could hear the ticking of the clock beside his bed.

"Well, he won't succeed."

Lee nodded as the door flew open and Ted's parents came in, chattering like children. "Oh, Ted," said his mother, rushing over and kissing him, "we're so glad you're okay."

"The doctor says it was a very slight concussion," said his father, "and the cut wasn't very deep. You won't even need stitches. A couple of days' rest, and you'll be out of here."

"That's good news," said Ted.

"I'll say it is," said his father. "We knew you were some rider. We had no idea you'd be in for this kind of a shock."

Ted glanced at Lee. "Neither did I."

"It was unbelievable," said his mother. "If Nelly hadn't slipped, you would have won the race."

"It must have been very frustrating for you," said his father. "To be that close and have it get away."

"It was," said Ted. "Very."

So this was how Jack's treachery would be remembered. He wanted to scream. Nelly hadn't slipped at all.

"Life isn't fair sometimes," said his father.

"No," said Ted. "It's not."

He lay back on his pillow. His parents began talking among themselves and then with Lee, who offered to take them to dinner at the mess hall. They thought that was a wonderful idea, if it wasn't a problem. They could come back afterward and say good-bye.

Time passed quietly, the shadows in the room lengthening, the dark pressing nearer. He tried not to think, tried to let his mind dance easily over surfaces without probing them. He was sore, sore everywhere, and his head hurt. But at least he was coming out of this intact.

The door opened. It was Higg.

He came and sat on the bed, reminding Ted of another evening and sitting on another bed to talk, In the half-light, Higg's face looked drawn. Had he come to apologize, to admit at last he was wrong about Jack? Had he come to recognize just how evil Jack was?

Ted forced himself to sit up. "At least I won you *one*."

"Ted," said Higg, "I'm really sorry this happened."

"Thanks. I appreciate that."

"You were so close to winning. It was such a nasty break."

So he didn't know the truth, or was denying it. Ted was shocked.

"It wasn't a nasty break. Jack hit me with his crop."

Higg took this in. His hand moved to the pipe in his breast pocket. He said sternly, "Are you accusing Jack of—"

"Yes," said Ted. "That's exactly what I'm doing."

He shouldn't have cut Higg off. It was as bad as saying Jack wanted to kill him. It made him seem irrational, a little crazy.

"I think you're being unjust," said Higg.

"I'm sorry you think that, sir."

"I'd still like to bring you two together. It might help, particularly after what's happened."

"I don't think so. I don't think Jack would come."

"He might. You underestimate him."

It was all Ted could do not to laugh. Bandages, bruises, nothing made any difference. "Yes, sir," he said, "you're probably right. I do underestimate him."

"Well," said Higg, "let's see how things go. In the meanwhile, I'm just glad you weren't badly hurt."

He stood up. At that moment T. R. Bruce appeared.

"How's the patient?"

"Seems pretty good to me," said Higg. "You know our Ted. He'll come through anything and still be tops."

"That's for sure," said Mr. Bruce.

"See you at dinner," said Higg.

"Yes, of course," said Mr. Bruce.

Ted felt as if he were witnessing some kind of verbal ballet. Or was it just two adults trying to be polite?

As the door closed behind Higg, Mr. Bruce said, "Well, you sure are popular."

Ted shrugged. "Just part of my charm."

"I assume your parents have given you the doctor's report."

"They have."

"Ted, I don't know what to say. I—"

Was this going to be the moment then? Mr. Bruce was in the center of the room, shadows collecting in his eyes.

"It's just that I wanted to tell you what great courage you showed. The race you ran was exceptional. You, more than anyone, have defined what it means to be a Cherokee camper. Regardless of the outcome, I'm proud, terribly proud, to have you here."

Ted took a deep breath and let it go. So there would be no moment of recognition then, no denial of Jack's right to hurt, no chance to set the record straight. Whatever else Mr. Bruce might have to say, it would all be meaningless.

Twenty

Around midnight, just three days after he'd left the infirmary, Ted was rolled out of bed. He hit the floor hard, instantly feeling every bruise on his body. No one in the cabin woke up, or at least no one was ready to admit he had. Two figures in wolf masks dragged him out the door.

Outside he was handed his clothes: jeans and a sweatshirt, sneakers. He dressed hurriedly, the night air chilling him, the dew wetting his feet as he struggled into his socks. When he was ready, he was blindfolded.

The blindfold shocked him into thought. Was Jack up to more tricks? The wolf masks seemed sort of official, like something to do with the Tribe. But surely Jack was part of the Tribe as well. . . .

"What's going on?" he asked.

He was surprised by the loudness of his voice.

One of the masked figures put a hand over his mouth. "No talking. Follow us."

They spun him around and led him away. High grass. A dirt road. He knew they were heading toward the riding field.

He didn't know exactly where, though, until the stream of water hit him in the face. His first reaction was: Not again. Couldn't you be more original? After that he just felt chilled and soggy.

He was left to stand by the watering trough. Then, suddenly, he was grabbed by both arms, dragged over to the road, and dumped in the back seat of a car.

Doors slammed. The car moved out. But they couldn't have gone more than a mile when it stopped. The same hands pulled him to his feet.

"We're going for a walk in the woods," someone said. "Be careful where you put your feet."

That was nice of them. A little word of warning to the prisoner. Would they let him know before Jack hit him over the head? It looked as if Lee had been wrong in his assessment of things.

They must have walked for about ten minutes, Ted feeling his way through the undergrowth and over roots and puddles. His wet jeans swished as he moved. The water oozed out of his sneakers.

Finally they stopped. Someone pushed Ted down. He would have sat willingly, had he been asked. Someone else pulled off the blindfold.

He was seated under a pine tree on a bed of pine needles. Four figures in wolf masks stood over him. One threw him a blanket. Another spoke.

"You will spend the night here. You will not take off your clothes or move from this spot. We will be watching."

"What is this all about?" Ted asked.

"No one said you could talk."

He huddled under the blanket, wishing it were warmer and his clothes weren't so wet. The woods weren't familiar, but they hadn't driven far enough for them not to be close to camp. At least they'd given him pine needles to lie on.

This couldn't just be Jack. It had to be the Tribe. The question was, what did the Tribe have in mind?

Lying on his side was the most comfortable position to be in. He could smell the sweet, strong scent of the pine needles best that way, too. His body heat was starting to dry his clothes. Eventually he fell asleep. It didn't feel like sleep, but it was.

The sun woke him. His clothes were almost dry, his sneakers still damp but not too disgusting. The woods were deep, mostly birch and oak. Nothing was more familiar than the night before.

Almost at once the four masked figures appeared. The masks were so elaborate, he couldn't recognize anyone.

He was blindfolded again. Then the same person who had spoken last night said, "We hope you had a good sleep."

"Oh, yes," said Ted. "Just like a luxury hotel. I could have used more heat, but I understand there are problems with the boiler."

The speaker laughed. "We're glad you were pleased. Because members of the Cherokee Tribe are meant to be tough. And if you get through today's initiation, you will be one of us."

There was a pause.

"Open your mouth," said the speaker.

Ted did as he was told. A piece of rounded wood was jammed between his teeth. Immediately he began to salivate.

"You will wear this bit all day. For every word spoken, you will get a notch. Six notches, and you are disqualified."

They marched him off. This time, perhaps because it was daylight and they had no trouble seeing, they were less concerned about his safety. He stumbled several times before they stopped.

The blindfold was removed. They were in a clearing,

and beyond the clearing was a deep pit, obviously the remains of Oliver Turpin's quarry. After Turpin's death on the Old Glory Road, the quarry had closed down. What use could the Tribe have found for it?

A small shack was at the edge of the woods. Two of the masked Tribe members led him there.

At one end was a fireplace flanked by two derelict wicker chairs. Over the mantle a banner, in green and gold, said: Cherokee Tribe. At the other end an improvised kitchen displayed a hot plate, a half-refrigerator, and a sink full of dirty dishes. In the middle was a picnic table, complete with benches. At the table, guarded by two masked Tribe members and wearing bits exactly like his, were Bob Colter and Lee.

Bob Colter was the friendly, barrel-chested kid Ted had first spoken to that night on the Old Glory Road. How long ago that seemed. The two masked Tribe members looked suspiciously like Hambone and Tim.

Ted was pushed into a seat at the table. He shared a look with Lee, half-smile, half-grimace.

A plate and a glass were dumped in front of him. On the plate: one cornflake, a fragment of scrambled egg, and a crumb of toast. In the glass: salt water.

"Enjoy your breakfast," said the Tribe member who had spoken before. "Remember, you must finish everything."

He practically inhaled the tiny bits of food. When he'd finally choked down the salt water, he was thirsty. Of course. That was the point.

Bits in mouths, the three of them were led out to the quarry. At the bottom was a large pile of horse manure.

162

They were given wheelbarrows to take down and fill. Then, one at a time, each was supposed to wheel his load up the side and drop it on the heads of the others.

This had to be a Jack Dunn idea.

All morning long, Ted, Lee, and Bob hauled manure and dumped it on one another. They got hungrier and thirstier. Their hair and their not-quite-dry clothes were covered in lots of little pieces—as well as the stink—of fresh manure.

Then it was time for lunch. One microscopic piece of charred roast beef. One string bean. One slice of apple. A large glass of fresh salt water.

"All right, guys," they heard as they finished. "Back to work."

By afternoon it was sunny and very hot. As they worked, perspiration seeped through their clothes. It got so horrible, they could hardly go on.

Ted had noticed that one of the guards was being especially nasty to Lee and him. When Ted dragged his wheelbarrow up the slope, the guard kicked sand in his face. When Lee was on his way down, the guard threw clots of dirt at the back of his neck. He did nothing to Bob.

Ted was sure the guard was Ricky Dunn.

Finally it was too much. He threw down the wheelbarrow and pulled the bit out of his mouth. "Shit! Cut it out!" he yelled.

The guard walked forward and pushed him down. The grin on his wolf mask made him look particularly diabolical. "You just got yourself four notches."

He took the bit out of Ted's hand, carved the notches

with a pocket knife, and handed it back. "I think you'd better be careful. Unless you want to blow this."

Should he care? Jack was doing it to him again. He had to see it through.

For the rest of the afternoon, he took what came. Sand, mud, pebbles—it didn't matter. Up and down they all went. The manure raining on their heads. Their mouths so parched they kept sucking on their bits.

At sundown there was an announcement. "Congratulations. You have all passed the test. You will now be formally inducted into the Cherokee Tribe."

Two masked Tribe members led them through the woods. Coming around a corner, they were told to squat and wait. "The old ceremonial grounds are up ahead," said one of their guides. "You will be called one by one."

Almost on cue, a voice said, "Bob Colter, please."

"Wish me luck," said Bob.

They did. A few minutes later they heard a gasp, a scream, and crying.

"Ted Jenner, please," came the voice.

Ted shook hands with Lee. He marched off between two wolf masks.

They entered another clearing, this one small and surrounded by log benches. In the middle was a fire, glowing brightly in the gathering dusk. Beside the fire was a totem pole, faces one on top of the other, leering in the flames.

On one of the log benches sat Bob Colter, head in his hands, sobbing. On others sat assorted Tribe members, now without their masks. There was Hambone. There was Ricky. There was Tim. Crouched beside the fire, holding a stick with a red-hot tip, was Jack Dunn.

164

Jack stood up. He was dressed in buckskin and the same headdress he had worn to burn the covered wagon. He flashed his familiar grin. "Welcome to the Cherokee Tribe. I, the Chief, await you."

Terrific, thought Ted. As if there had been any doubt.

He was pushed over to the totem pole and tied to it, hands behind his back. He might have resisted, but there wasn't time. Jack faced him.

"As a symbol of your induction into the Tribe, the greatest of honors at Camp Cherokee, I am going to brand you on the forehead. It will hurt, but you will love it."

"I don't think so," said Ted.

"This time you really have no choice."

Jack walked forward, the point on the stick glowing in his hand. With every step, Ted strained at the rope.

Jack grinned. He brought the hot stick to within an inch of Ted's forehead. "I hope you're going to enjoy this. I know I am."

Ted stared into Jack's eyes. In one motion, Jack went to brand Ted's forehead, then reached down and touched the spot with a piece of cold charcoal instead.

Jack laughed. "You thought I'd do it, didn't you?"

"Jack, nothing you could do would ever surprise me."

Jack scowled. "Now scream and pretend to cry, so we can scare Lee."

"No," said Ted. "I won't."

"You what?"

"You heard me. You're a piece of shit, Jack, and I won't do anything you tell me to do. You've hurt a lot of people at this camp, and it's about time someone stopped you!"

Jack turned dark red. His eyes glowed. His voice became

a hiss. "You have the nerve to speak like this to me? To me, Jack Dunn, Chief of the Cherokee Tribe? Well, let me tell you something, boy. I know you're not coming back next year. I know you don't care about Cherokee tradition. I only had you and Lee inducted because I wanted to rub your noses in more shit. And I've been waiting all day to give you some myself!"

He stripped off his belt and slashed Ted across the face.

The movement was so unexpected, Ted didn't even duck. "Oh," he said, feeling the sharp sting of the leather and the rip of the buckle.

But Jack wasn't finished. He picked up another stick and began heating it in the fire. At that moment Tim and Ricky rushed up and found sticks themselves.

"Let's get him," said Tim. "Let's really do it! I've waited so long!"

The sticks started to glow. Jack stood up, ready.

Until then, the other Tribe members had remained in their seats, not quite believing what they were seeing. Now Hambone raced across the circle, whirled Jack around, and flattened him with one punch. Others grabbed Tim and Ricky and dragged them away.

Hambone pointed down at Jack. "I want you out of this camp by tonight. I don't care what excuse you give. If you're not gone, the Cherokee Tribe will make sure you are."

Jack struggled to his knees. He tried to stand. Hambone knocked him down again.

"Okay," Jack said, "okay."

Twenty-one

They were walking back to camp along the Old Glory Road. It was dark, but the moon was bright enough.

"So how does it feel to be a member of the Cherokee Tribe?" Ted asked.

"I'm not sure," said Lee. "I never got my ceremonial brand."

"I wouldn't be too upset. Jack was only just getting started when Hambone creamed him."

"Tim and Ricky got in on it, too, I hear."

"That was the saddest part. I knew Tim had it in for me. I didn't know it was that bad."

"You think Jack's really going to go?"

"I think so. The Tribe won't let him stay."

"It's hard to believe. Can't you just see him coming up to Mr. Bruce with some weird explanation?"

"Yeah. Excuse me, Mr. Bruce, I've suddenly been overtaken by this—well, it's a serious mental illness—and I—"

Lee laughed. "And I thought Jack had finished with you."

"You should have known better. How many years was he roasting your ass?"

"Five."

"No one could accuse Jack Dunn of being a quitter."

"I still can't figure out why he did any of it. All that

violence and putting people down. How could you enjoy being like that? Why would you want to *do* things like that?"

"Who knows? I bet he doesn't even know. But he had so much power. I guess when you can do anything you want and a certain kind of attitude supports you, there's always the temptation to go one step further."

"It's how he ever got the power that's so weird."

"I don't think we'll ever know the real answer to that. I don't think there is an answer."

"Well, what do you say? With Jack out of the picture, are you coming back next year?"

"No."

"Even though you're going to win best camper?"

"Is that true?"

"Odds-on favorite."

"Tim will be so pleased."

"You could be a C.I.T."

"A counselor-in-training here? You've got to be kidding. No way."

"Me neither."

"Me neither," said a familiar voice. The bushes parted. "Hambone!" Ted and Lee both said at once.

"Yeah," said Hambone, "I thought you guys could use some company. You never know what might pop out of the woods this late at night."

"I never had a chance to thank you," said Ted.

"No thanks necessary. I'm just amazed it took me so long to figure it all out. You kept telling me. I just wouldn't believe you."

"You were there when it counted."

"Yeah. When the thought finally penetrates the brain, everything else comes with it."

168

"Are you really not coming back next summer?" Lee asked.

"I don't think so. Jack's kind of soured me on this place."

"Well," said Ted, "maybe we can all do something else together."

"Sounds good," said Hambone.

"I'll be there," said Lee.

"Anyhow," said Ted, "we've got to stay friends."

They had passed the gully of the Old Glory Road and were climbing the hill to the riding field. They stopped and clasped hands, three together, like the spokes of a wheel.

"Friends," said Hambone.

"Friends," said Lee.

"Friends," said Ted.

About the Author

STEVEN KROLL grew up in New York City and graduated with a degree in history and literature from Harvard College. He has been an editor and a book reviewer, and now writes full time at his home in New York City. He is the author of many books for young readers, including *The Biggest Pumpkin Ever*, *Santa's Crash-Bang Christmas* and *That Makes Me Mad!* His first novel for young adults, *Take It Easy!*, is also a Point paperback.